BEACH READING

Full of lively characters and wacky coincidence, this page-turning series aims to become the *Tales of the City* of the new millennium. In the popular imagination, the heyday of gay life is long gone, washed away by AIDS. But in this love song to San Francisco, Mark Abramson gives the lie to that myth, revealing the joy that still inheres to life in the City by the Bay. The quirky charm of San Francisco is alive and well, and living in the pages of *Beach Reading*.

—Lewis DeSimone, author of *Chemistry*

The first entry in Mark Abramson's **Beach Reading Series** pits a brokenhearted, endearing, bar-hopping Castro hero against a seething homophobe all set against the backdrop of a colossal dance party honoring 80s-legend Sylvester. What could be more fun?!

You won't need sand and surf to enjoy this sunny, campy, quick-witted gem. A sheer delight."

—Jim Piechota, *Bay Area Reporter*

Beach Reading

Mark Abramson

Lethe Press
Maple Shade, NJ

Printed in the United States of America
Book Design by Toby Johnson
Cover Design by Bob Meadows

Published as a trade paperback original
by Lethe Press, 118 Heritage Avenue, Maple Shade, NJ 08052.
First U.S. edition, 2008
ISBN 1-59021-139-1   ISBN-13   978-1-59021-139-7

Library of Congress Cataloging-in-Publication Data

Abramson, Mark, 1952-
    Beach reading / Mark Abramson. -- 1st U.S. ed.
        p. cm.
    ISBN-13: 978-1-59021-139-7 (trade pbk.)
    ISBN-10: 1-59021-139-1 (trade pbk.)
    1. Gay and lesbian dance parties--Fiction. 2. Gay men--
Fiction. 3. San Francisco (Calif.)--Fiction. 4. Evangelists--Fiction. 5.
Homophobia--Fiction. I. Title.
    PS3601.B758B43 2008
    813'.6--dc22
                                        2008021820

D espite any resemblance to living and/or historical figures, all characters mentioned or appearing in *Beach Reading* are fictitious except Sylvester, Two Tons o' Fun, former Mayor Willie Brown, Mavis, Jon Carroll, Leah Garchik, Harvey Milk, Dianne Feinstein, Dan White, Wayne Friday, Carol Doda, Jan Wahl and Dame Edna Everage, who is only partially fictitious.

Prologue

Sunday morning in the financial district Corey Donatelli thought he saw a spaceship from the window of the limousine. It scattered shards of reflected sunlight across the Transamerica Pyramid and the book-shaped towers of the Embarcadero Center. Corey asked his uncle to have the driver stop right there on California Street where they lowered the tinted windows and looked up at an enormous mirror ball suspended from a helicopter. A biplane pulled a yellow banner across the blue sky. It read:

DANCE CELEBRATE REMEMBER
A Tribute to SYLVESTER'S birthday
Moscone Center SATURDAY

Corey had never heard of Sylvester, but he wanted to go. Today was his birthday; this was his first trip to San Francisco and everything had been perfect so far. They had taken a long ride along the waterfront, stopped for a Bloody Mary at

Fisherman's Wharf and now they were headed toward Castro Street for brunch at a place his uncle had heard about called Arts. Corey would also meet Tim Snow this morning, but unlike Tim, Corey was one of those gay men who could come to San Francisco for a visit and then go on about his life. So this isn't really Corey's story.

San Francisco dazzles most people who visit, but only some get trapped here. You might wonder if they'd turned their heads a moment sooner, like breaking their concentration away from the hypnotist's swaying bauble just in time, they might be able to go back where they came from. Tim Snow could never leave, but he enjoyed being caught here. He almost felt normal in San Francisco. He had longed to be normal ever since he was a boy and started seeing things the way his grandmother did. Tim hoped from those early inklings that clairvoyance, like his first excitement around other boys at the swimming pool, was something that would just go away if he ignored it hard enough. His grandmother had called it a gift, but it wasn't a present he'd asked for. Sometimes he tried to treat his unwanted psychic ability the way a handicapped person must learn to just get on with his life. So this is mostly Tim's story.

It is partly Artie's story, too. He and Arturo fell in love in Vietnam during the war and they got trapped in San Francisco afterward. Artie discovered a whole new life when he put on a dress and found his way to a stage in North Beach to regale the crowds of drunken tourists. After Finocchio's closed, it took him a few years to find a place on Castro Street where he fit in again.

They would all agree that if this isn't Ruth's story, she was an essential part of theirs. Ruth might have been trapped in San Francisco by the flower children in the 1960s when she was a student at Stanford. But she went back to Minnesota instead, got married and rescued her nephew Tim after his parents threw him out when they found out he was gay. Ruth always wanted to return, but she never found a good enough reason. When she came for a visit, not planning to stay, she was just in time to rescue her nephew once again.

Around the time of her divorce, Ruth sent Tim an obituary notice from the *Minneapolis Star and Tribune*. A farmer near Worthington died at 102 years old. He'd lived his whole life within fifteen miles of where he was born in the same house where he died. One day when he was a young man he rode a horse across the state line into Iowa, just so he could say that he'd been someplace, but he came right back. He knew where he belonged.

Tim asked her if she meant he should come back to Minnesota, but he'd missed her point entirely, which was not unusual for Tim. He inherited his grandmother's gift, but he couldn't see what was right in front of him. His Aunt Ruth had to explain that Tim's vision led him here because San Francisco was where he belonged.

Chapter 1

I t was 3:05pm when Tim Snow's last table showed signs they were getting ready to leave. He'd never seen these men in Arts before and he would have remembered them if they always took a limousine to brunch. Tim knew they were from out of town because one of them asked for an ashtray when they sat down. He couldn't remember a time when people still smoked in restaurants in California.

They were celebrating the youngest one's birthday and even suggested that Tim might make a good gift for the birthday boy. He'd enjoyed flirting, but was startled when the bald guy winked and said, "Meet us at The Eagle Tavern in a couple of hours. I'll make it worth your while."

"Hmmm, FBI... It looks like you're in trouble now, Tim!" Artie said when he processed the credit card behind the bar.

"Huh?" Tim usually paid little attention to his boss when he started rambling.

"Don't get too excited about handcuffs, dear. His initials spell FBI, that's all."

Tim was still smiling at the foursome and trying to accept their offer to meet them as mere flattery. He hadn't seen his tip yet. "What'd you say, Artie?"

"Nothing… hey, I knew they were running up quite a bar tab, but you sold them a bottle of our best champagne, too. Whatever you're doing, keep at it!"

"I'm not doing anything special, Artie," Tim protested. "It's the youngest one's birthday and they're visiting San Francisco for a long weekend. I offered him a slice of cake. I was going to stick a candle in it and ask Viv to play *Happy Birthday,* but she must be on another break. He declined, anyway—too many carbs, I suppose. He hardly touched his food, either. They must all be on a liquid diet."

"Hmmm… the birthday boy is a cutie, Tim."

"Never mind, Artie… you know I'm not into chicken."

"You could do worse," Artie persisted. "Besides, it might help you stop mooning over Jason if you'd get laid once in a while."

"I *do* get laid once in a while and I'm *not* mooning over Jason." Tim didn't want to talk about Jason, especially not at work. "When did you become such a matchmaker, anyway?"

"He's always trying to fix me up, too," said Jake, the other waiter. "Every time a guy comes in with a tattoo or any visible body piercing, Artie's trying to marry me off. Just because I like them on my own body, doesn't necessarily mean…"

"You better be careful, Jake," Tim interrupted. "I've heard of teenagers getting their braces stuck together when they kiss, but I'd hate for you to get your eyebrow ring tangled up in some hot stud's Prince Albert."

"Don't start with me, Tim. I'm not the one who chipped a tooth at Blow-Buddies."

"I don't want either of you two boys to start," Artie scolded. "I'm telling you Tim, I can't always arrange the schedule so that you and Jason never see each other. One of these days you'll have to work together again and you're going to have to get over this."

"Is that what you're doing? You're arranging the schedule to spare my feelings? Don't worry about me, Artie. I'm fine." Tim picked up a tray and went back to clear the glasses and coffee cups from his last table. He was feeling irritable now, but he smiled when he picked up the signed credit card slip and found the crisp hundred-dollar bill beneath it. Tim glanced up to see two of the men standing out on the sidewalk smoking cigarettes.

"Thanks for everything," Tim heard a shy voice behind him. It was the birthday boy coming out of the restroom. Judging from the way he walked, he'd either had too much to drink or his black leather boots were a birthday present he hadn't broken in yet.

"Happy birthday," Tim told him again, "and enjoy the rest of your stay in San Francisco."

"Won't I see you later? My uncle said you might be able to join us. I think we're headed someplace South of Market."

"Maybe..." Tim left it at that. He didn't want to encourage the kid. He was cute, but much too young for Tim's taste. Still... it had been a while. "Have fun."

"Thanks... bye..." The boy looked back at Tim as he headed toward the door.

"Will you look at that?" Tim said to Jake, who was resetting a nearby table with a clean linen tablecloth, wine glasses and double forks for the evening dinner shift.

"What is it, Tim? Did he leave you his phone number?"

"Better!" Tim held up the hundred-dollar bill so that Jake could see it, but not the rest of the room. "They asked me to meet them later, too."

"Are you going to? You should! That bald guy must be rich! I'd do him in a minute."

"No, it's the kid who was interested in me," Tim said. "I could go South of Market, I suppose. I'm not working tonight. I was going home to pay some bills and maybe call my Aunt Ruth in Minnesota. She's going through a messy divorce and sounds bummed out. I should do laundry, too."

Tim continued bussing the table and spotted a note under the FBI man's saucer. It read: *The birthday boy's name is Corey. If you can't join us at The Eagle, he's in room #2553 at the Marriott Hotel on 4th Street. I will make it worth your while.* The note was signed: *Uncle Fred.*

"Jeez!" Tim said to Artie. "That's twice he's used the phrase 'worth your while.' Uncle Fred wants to hire me for his nephew's birthday! The back pages of the gay papers are full of paid escorts. Why try to pick up a waiter?" Still, Tim was flattered. He unloaded the dirty glasses from the tray onto the bar and gave Artie the credit card slip.

"What? He hit on you and didn't even leave a tip? That's some nerve!" Artie placed the check on one pile and the credit card slip on another. He would take them to the office in a few minutes and balance the receipts from brunch. The end of the month was nearing and it showed by how little money the customers spent these days.

"They left a cash tip," Tim said with a smile, but he didn't tell Artie how much. The waiters traditionally gave the bartenders a percentage of their tips, but not when Artie was working behind the bar. As one of the owners, he wouldn't accept them. "I didn't mean to snap at you about Jason, Artie. I know you're just trying to spare my feelings, but you don't need to juggle the schedule on my account. Jason and I worked together before we slept together and there's no reason we can't work together again. Who knows? Maybe someday we'll be friends."

"'Attaboy!" Artie resumed his motherly stance. He did feel almost parental toward his employees, especially where Tim was concerned. "You and Jason were coming at each other from different directions. That doesn't make either of you the bad guy. You could maybe learn a thing or two from Jason, Tim."

"I hope you're right, Artie. I guess if I'm going to meet them I'd better stop at home and change into something more appropriate for South of Market on a Sunday afternoon."

"Maybe you've started learning a few things from Jason already."

Tim walked up Castro Street to 19th, around the corner and up the hill on Collingwood. Artie and Arturo were not only his bosses, but also his landlords. They lived on the top floor of their three-story Victorian apartment building and Tim lived on the bottom. Tim glanced at the answering machine beside his bed, but the light wasn't blinking. There were a few e-mails on his computer, but they were mostly Spam. Nothing looked urgent or even very interesting.

He slipped out of his khaki slacks and the blue knit shirt that showed off his chest so well. Tim had always kept in good shape by running, but Jason had also gotten him into the habit of working out at the gym. As much as he dreaded his gym routine some days, he had to admit it paid off if he was getting hundred-dollar bills in his tips. These days he tried to schedule his trips to the gym to avoid running into Jason, especially in the showers. Tim didn't want to be reminded of how much he missed them being naked together.

He glanced toward the overflowing hamper in the corner and tossed his work clothes onto the pile. Laundry could wait. South of Market sounded like a better idea. He pulled off his socks and stepped into the shower, turning the water up as hot as it would go. The phone rang as soon as Tim wet his hair. The telephone could wait, too.

Tim imagined the smells of maple syrup and bacon sliding off his bare skin and swirling down the drain. He soaped and rinsed his armpits left, right, again and a third time. Whether or not he ended up with Corey the birthday boy, he might meet someone on a sunny Sunday afternoon in one of the South of Market bars. Tim envisioned himself naked on a bed in a luxurious hotel room above the fog at sunset stretching to raise his arms behind his head. He didn't want to have some hot guy's tongue slide across his chest to nuzzle his armpit and gag on the deodorant Tim wore to work that morning.

He toweled off in front of the full-length mirror on the bathroom door and shook the water out of his hair. He'd meant to get it cut this week, but hadn't found the time. It was getting to the length where it started to curl around his ears. He would either have to cut it soon or endure an awkward phase for a couple of weeks. Tim thought of when Jason once told him that he liked Tim's hair longer. He said it gave him something to hang onto. That did it. Jason was part of the past. Tim would get a haircut this week for sure.

He pressed the PLAY button on his answering machine, but whoever called hadn't left a message. T-shirt, Levi's, boots and a jacket over one shoulder and he was ready to hit the streets, the gutters, or whatever waited out there. Tim's hair still wasn't quite dry, but he pulled on a baseball cap, one that Jason had bought him on Castro Street when they first started seeing each other. It was black with the word **COLT** embroidered across the front in gold letters. Tim grabbed his keys, took one more glance in the mirror and decided that he looked just fine.

Chapter 2

Tim boarded a vintage streetcar on 17th Street outside the Twin Peaks bar. He sat in one of the single seats behind the driver and picked up a brochure that told him the St. Louis Car Company had built this vehicle in 1948 and its colors—green and cream with a black stripe—represented the Louisville Railway, although it had never actually been used in Kentucky. Tim took a deep breath and tucked the brochure in his pocket. He might read it later, but he wasn't in the mood right now. He glanced at the headline of a newspaper someone had left on the seat: *Reverend Arlo Montgomery to bring his anti-gay crusade to San Francisco.* Tim wasn't in the mood for reading the news either, and besides, he had the same paper at home on his kitchen table.

The streetcar's windows were wide open and the smells of Orphan Andy's 24-hour diner mingled with the sweet warm chocolate and almonds from the cookie store, coffee from further down the street and even popcorn from the matinee at the Castro Theatre. Some days Tim liked one smell or another, but all of them at once were overpowering. The smell of Orphan Andy's deep-fryer reminded him of the Minnesota State Fair in St. Paul. His dad took Tim and the boy next-door when they were kids and Tim remembered knowing he would be sick before he even got to the rides—the whole reason for the State Fair — but he couldn't turn down a corn-dog, funnel cake, cotton candy and a deep-fried banana.

Living in San Francisco reminded Tim of being a kid at the fair. No matter how full he was, it was hard to say no. There was always something right around the next corner that might not be good for him, but he had to try it at least once anyway.

At Church Street Tim glanced to his left toward the Safeway supermarket and thought of something Jake said earlier at work: "Whenever I don't have any luck at the bars, I head over to Safeway after-hours. You should try it, Tim. They're open all night. I just put a can of Crisco in my shopping cart and push it up and down the aisles until I meet someone. The produce section is best at that hour." The waiters at Arts sometimes teased each other, but Jake was okay, always in a good mood.

Now Tim noticed an old lady boarding the streetcar. Grocery bags in both hands weighed her down. She reminded Tim of his grandmother, who died when he was about eight years old. Tim's grandmother probably wasn't as old as this woman, but most grown-ups looked ancient to a kid that age.

Tim kept a framed picture of his grandmother next to his bed. She sat with her arm around him on a blue and green plaid blanket beside the lake in Powderhorn Park in Minneapolis. It was the Fourth of July and they were waiting to hear the Symphony play the 1812 Overture and watch fireworks from that spot. Tim had on red swim trunks and he was holding a tiny American flag. He had a bandage on the big toe of his left foot. He remembered the swim trunks, but not how he hurt his toe. His family went to Powderhorn Park every year on the Fourth until the summer he turned 16 and they threw him out, but he didn't want to think about any of that right now.

He was in San Francisco, now. More than twenty years had evaporated since that picture was taken. Nothing could pull him back there. He was happier now. Things were better here, in spite of having been dumped by Jason. He had no reason to dwell on the past. Then the streetcar lurched and the old lady lunged toward him. Tim tried to brace her fall, but she landed half-way in his lap. "Hello-o-o…" she said with a giggle. "I'm so terribly sorry, young man."

"Are you all right? Let me help you… your groceries…" Tim propped her up in the single seat ahead of his. The grocery bags were intact, but oranges rolled across the floor. Other passengers reached beneath their feet to collect them and Tim put them back among the carrots, celery, and a baguette of sourdough bread.

"Thank you so much. Why, I don't even know your name, but you're awfully kind. I'm Vanessa Caen, no relation to Herb, though I did meet him at a party once when I was here to visit my little brother. He was a charming man, I thought… Herb Caen, I mean."

"My name is Tim… Tim Snow. Are you sure you're all right?"

"I think so, Timothy Snow. Tim *is* short for Timothy, isn't it? It's very nice to meet you. I'm more embarrassed than injured, I'm sure, but my pride doesn't take as long to heal as a broken bone would at my age. I must be more careful when riding on these streetcar contraptions or else I need to wear more sensible shoes in San Francisco."

Tim looked down at her shoes. They were in the style of men's wing-tips, but had heels about two inches high made of red and gold lamé with black ankle straps and tiny black bows across each toe. Everything she wore was red and gold and trimmed in black. Her red skirt showed off shapely legs for a woman her age. She wore a frilly red blouse and a gold hat over short silver curls. She might have been dressed to go dancing rather than the supermarket. Tim thought maybe she'd been to church since it was Sunday. "I hope you don't think I make a habit of throwing myself into the arms of handsome young strangers!" she went on. "Thank you so much."

"It's no trouble at all, Miss Caen. How far do you have to go?"

"Mrs. Caen," she corrected. "I'm a widow. But please call me Vanessa. I'm riding this to 8th Street. My brother Harley lives near there."

"Harvey?" Tim asked. He was only half listening. He had his eye on a man who was boarding the streetcar. Tim thought he might have been someone he'd brought home to bed once, but that wasn't it. He must have been a recent customer at Arts who Tim had waited on.

"No, my brother's name is Harley—like the motorcycle— Harley Davidson, although his last name is Wagner, the same as my maiden name—Vanessa Wagner. Harley thought about changing his name to Harley Davidson, but he never got around to it. I think that would have been a bit much, don't you? He lives on Clementina. It's one of those little alley streets before Folsom. He hasn't been very well, I'm afraid. That's why I've come to San Francisco, to help him get used to being home from the hospital again. And you, Timothy, where are you headed?"

"I'm meeting some friends at a bar." Tim felt a pang of guilt for lying. They weren't friends. He didn't even know Corey and his uncle and those other two guys. Why was he stretching the truth for this old lady? He didn't know her either. Maybe it was because she reminded him of his grandmother. It was conceivable that he *might* run into some friends South of Market and it would be the truth. Or he might *become* friends with someone he would meet that day.

Maybe he felt guilty about going to a bar. His grandmother had probably never set foot inside a bar in her entire life and certainly not a gay bar, but this woman on the streetcar was a stranger. Where was this guilt coming from? Tim thought he must be stoned, but then he remembered he was out of grass. He'd been thinking about looking for a roach to smoke when he got out of the shower, but he knew it was no use.

"I could get off at 8th Street and help you," Tim said, hoping to be forgiven for whatever gnawed at the guilty part of his brain. Maybe he felt guilty about sex. Not only had Corey come on to him, but the older guy, Uncle Fred, had offered Tim money. No one had ever offered Tim money for sex before. He'd never considered such a thing. It was flattering, he supposed, but really…

"That's very kind of you, but I'm sure I'll be fine," the old lady named Vanessa said. "I'd hate for you to go out of your way on account of me."

Tim wasn't even interested in the birthday boy—Corey. The kid was cute enough, all right, but Tim was more interested in guys at least his own age or a few years older. "Don't mention it," he said and noticed that the old lady was still smiling at him.

He liked meeting men who wore San Francisco on their faces and in their walk. He liked the sort of men who were sure of themselves, who had been around. He admired the survivors, the men who might teach him a thing or two. In spite of his visions or maybe because of them, Tim understood since he was a little boy that there would be people waiting out there in the world to teach him things. Tim didn't feel that he was experienced enough to be anyone else's teacher unless they needed a lesson in how to wait tables and flirt. He could teach master classes in both of those.

Tim's fingertips felt for the hundred-dollar bill inside his pocket. Why hadn't he broken it at the restaurant or left it at home? He had plenty of smaller bills on his dresser. He had his MUNI pass with him, but even if he got drunk and splurged on a cab ride home from South of Market, he wouldn't need a hundred dollars in cash.

"My brother Harley has one of those little carts on two wheels," Vanessa said. "He told me I should take it when I go shopping. I walk by it every day, standing there in the entry beneath the coat hooks. I just don't want to look like an old lady, you know?"

"But you…" Tim started.

"Don't say it! I know I *am* an old lady, but I don't want to feel like one," she insisted. "If I allow myself to look like an old lady I'll *feel* like one and I am determined to avoid that at all costs."

"All I meant is that you should be more careful," Tim said. "If you break a leg on the streetcar you won't be much help to your brother."

"You are not only a kind and helpful young man, but a very sensible one, too. Here… this is my stop… oh… my ankle!"

"Here, let me help you," Tim stood up before she could. "It's on my way, really."

Tim gathered her grocery bags in one hand, pulled the cord with the other and managed to help her up at the same time. She leaned on his free arm, limping slightly as they exited by the front door, watched for inbound traffic on Market Street and crossed over to the curb.

Tim wasn't familiar with Clementina Street. It wasn't really a street at all, but one of those alleys that run haphazardly through the maze of South of Market streets. Some go straight for several blocks and others run for only a few yards, stop, and then start up again where you'd least expect them. Tim's fingers were sore from the handles of so many grocery bags in his left hand while he helped Vanessa with his right. When they stopped at the red light at Howard Street, he readjusted his grip to get the circulation moving again. She insisted on taking one of the lighter bags in her right hand. Her body's weight on him was barely noticeable. By the time she let go of Tim's arm to search in her red and gold purse for keys, she seemed to be walking better, too.

"Here's our door, Timothy," she told him as she let go. He transferred the groceries to his other hand and flexed his left hand's fingers a few times. The building was more modern than the Victorians on either side of it. Tim guessed it was built in the 1960s, but he didn't know much about architecture.

He noticed a small stenciled logo on the door that faced street level and asked her, "Is this some kind of business?"

"There's a print shop on the bottom floors," Vanessa explained. "They use the middle floors for storage and that makes it nice and quiet on top. Harley has rented to them for years. Bill owned the building originally. Here we are, now." The elevator was barely large enough for the two of them and her groceries, which Tim set on the floor. She pushed a button and the elevator scraped slowly upward in its shaft.

"Bill was Harley's... What do you call it? Husband, I guess. Harley's a widow too, like me. Widower, I should say," she corrected herself. "What differences do labels make, I wonder? You could call a stone a thistle or a thorn a lollipop, but a rose is a rose... How does that saying go?"

"I'm not sure I know." Tim tried to be polite, but now he began to feel the afternoon slipping away from him. He wondered what he was doing in a noisy old elevator with this well-dressed, but peculiar old woman. The more he listened to Vanessa Caen, the less she reminded him of his grandmother.

He was curious about his grandmother because he'd inherited her gift, but she died before he understood what it meant. The gift hadn't come with instructions and no one wanted to talk about it, as if they were ashamed of her. So she remained in a photograph on a plaid blanket and he could only guess what mysteries might exist beyond that. Now he couldn't remember whether his grandmother's dress was red or were his swimming trunks the red in the picture? Maybe they were blue and her dress was gray. He wanted to go straight home and look at the picture again, but he was here now. The picture would wait. Even if Tim had the chance to go back to that moment in time, he might choose to know more about the little boy in the swim trunks than the old lady with her arm around him. Why was there a bandage on his toe? Did it hurt much? He could think of dozens of questions, but the elevator jerked and stopped at the top of the shaft. Tim closed his eyes to concentrate. More than twenty years had passed. The toe on that foot was inside these leather boots in San Francisco now and he knew there wasn't even a scar left on it.

"Here we are, then. Watch your step, Timothy Snow." Vanessa led the way into the home of her brother. "Harley knows how to make the elevator land evenly with the floor, but I haven't learned the secret. I don't mind stepping up or down a bit. I can take one little step. It's better than carrying things up all those flights of stairs."

Tim saw the coat hooks and the "old-lady" cart she mentioned earlier, so he knew that much was true, not that he had reason to doubt her. His fingers were burning and in his opinion, this was one old lady who should swallow her pride and use the darned cart, but it wasn't his business to say so. They turned a corner into a bright room that looked like a greenhouse. It had tall windows and skylights, flowering trees and hanging plants from floor to ceiling. One wall was covered in shelves of orchids with at least half of them in full bloom.

"Just set everything down on the table there, if you don't mind, Timothy."

Tim relieved himself of the grocery bags and looked around. "It must be hard work taking care of all these plants."

"Oh, I couldn't. I'd kill them, I'm sure. Harley hires someone to come in all the time—a young fellow who lives nearby. Harley used to take care of them all by himself, but now he just admires them when he can. He must be asleep or he'd be out here to see who I'm talking to. I don't know how to thank you enough for your help, Timothy. Would you like a cup of tea?"

"No, thanks, I…"

"Perhaps a glass of iced tea, instead. I believe you said you were on your way to meet some friends at a bar. Harley says there used to be a lot of bars for men in this neighborhood, but not so many these days. Maybe you'd like a cold beer or a drink? We have liquor too, if I can figure out how to open this cabinet."

Tim watched Vanessa's tiny shoes press levers near the floor in one corner of this room that opened into a kitchen. One pedal made the refrigerator door pop open, so she reached inside a grocery bag and found a carton of milk to place on the shelf. It seemed as if she couldn't bear to have opened it by mistake, so rather than waste the motion she put the milk away. She shoved the door shut with her hip, although there must have been other things in those bags that needed to be refrigerated.

"Would you like some marijuana instead? It's medicinal! Harley has permission from his doctor to grow it. I can show you the plants."

Tim wasn't sure what to say. He wanted to smoke a joint when he left home, but he didn't have any. He already felt stoned, not like the feelings he got around precognition—that usually came to him in his dreams, anyway—but Tim had a sense that in spite of Vanessa's sickly brother, he was in a place with a lot of life in it.

Vanessa went back to work on the pedals and discovered one that turned on a ceiling fan. "Well, that's just fine," she said with a laugh. "It wasn't what I was aiming for, but I've been trying to turn on that fan for days. One of these levers opens the liquor cabinet, I'm sure of it."

"I don't need a drink," Tim said. "I could use a glass of water if it's no trouble and then I should be on my way."

"Of course, of course." She glanced up at the cupboard and back down at the mysterious pedals. She spied a clean glass resting on the dish drainer next to the sink. "Here we are. I know there's a pitcher of good cold filtered water in the refrigerator and that was this one, wasn't it?" She pressed her red and gold toe down at the same place where she started and triumphantly poured a glass of water for Tim. "Voila!"

"Thank you," Tim smiled and took a sip. It was what he needed. He could order a beer when he got to the Lone Star or the Eagle or maybe the Powerhouse. Maybe he'd have a real drink later, depending on who was working. Some bartenders made better drinks than others.

"The next time Harley is up and about, I'll ask him how to open the liquor cabinet. It's behind those mirrors by the sink. I've seen it open for parties and there's going to be one soon. I'll get you an invitation, Timothy. What a good idea! You will come, won't you? That's how I can repay you for your kindness."

"It's all right, really. It was on my way and you hurt your foot. How is your foot, now? Is it better?"

"I think so," she looked down at it as if she had forgotten. "Let me show you the deck before you go. We have the whole rooftop, right through this door. And you mustn't say no to the party." She led the way between a pair of potted Schefflera plants while she removed her hat and set it on a table inside the door.

"Maybe if I'm not working I could come by for a little while."

"This is really very nice and quite strong stuff, too." Tim didn't see her pick up the joint, but once they reached the deck, she lifted it to her lips and lit it with a small jeweled lighter. She took a hit and handed it to Tim.

"This deck is amazing!" Tim took the joint from her tiny hand. There were more trees out here, plus a fountain and a pond of fat golden koi. Vanessa sat down on a bench and patted the seat beside her.

"There's a terrific view of those hills on a clear day. Today it was clear earlier, but the fog is coming in like a big white fur piece. Look! You can see the top of that tower that looks like a ship."

Tim looked west toward Twin Peaks and Mt. Sutro and thought he must be overly stoned now. He had to be hallucinating because he thought he saw something sparkling emerge from the clouds. It looked like the biggest mirror ball he had ever seen and it was suspended from the bottom of a helicopter. The old lady saw it, too. "Look, Timothy! Isn't that pretty? They must be doing something gay."

Tim took another hit off the joint and handed it back. He wasn't sure how Vanessa meant the word *gay*, but the mirror ball was heading in the direction of Castro Street and it would soon be visible to everyone who was out and about on this Sunday afternoon. Now he saw a biplane coming out of the bank of clouds behind the helicopter. It was too far away for him to read the advertising banner, but Tim was sure he would hear all about it very soon.

Chapter 3

Stoned! Tim said goodbye to the strange old lady and she closed the door to his cage. No, it wasn't a cage, but an elevator and he felt a moment of panic as it fell. Tim had no sense of time, but he was sure he would die when it hit the bottom. He didn't know how far it was but when it landed he was alive and he couldn't remember the difference between yards and inches anyway. That started him laughing, but not until the cage door opened and he stepped out into fresh air. He was thrilled to be alive and laughing. He must be in San Francisco even though nothing looked familiar.

Tim walked down 8th Street toward Folsom. He was so stoned that it felt like his hat was squeezing his temples and he wanted to rush home and shave off all his hair. But he wasn't wearing his hat! It was his favorite baseball cap and he must have taken if off, but where and when? He didn't even know where he was or how he had gotten to this point. Did she say something about the grass being medicinal? She must

29

have meant medical. Tim thought it was "medicinal" enough to call for a doctor. He was so lost he might as well be walking down Lake Street in Minneapolis, laughing, but he couldn't remember laughing his way down Lake Street. His hat didn't matter right now.

He needed a drink. Or did he need more water? He had been drinking water, hadn't he? Yes, it was cool and liquid and very blue… or was it the glass that was blue? Tim thought he might die of thirst and now he was standing outside a bar. Men smoked cigarettes near the doorway. Tim looked at his watch. It was just past five. There was plenty of time to do whatever he had planned, if only he could remember what it was.

"Hey, you got a light, man?" someone asked. Tim reached inside his breast pocket. Even though he didn't smoke cigarettes, he often carried a lighter or matches for a joint. His pocket felt full. There were matches, all right, and a couple of joints, too. Now he remembered when the old lady pressed them into his hand. Vanessa, that was her name, but she was nothing like his grandmother. It didn't matter now. Tim handed the matches to the scruffy man.

"Where'd you get them matches, man?" he asked Tim. "The Trench hasn't been there for at least twenty years! That place was hella wild—just up the street there." He pointed, but Tim wasn't sure where. "The Club Baths was in that gray one on the corner of 8th and Howard and the Trench yewsta be on the other side farther up towards Market." Tim was distracted when he thought he heard a helicopter again, but he couldn't see it.

"I don't know," Tim said. "Someone gave them to me, I guess. I can't remember."

"You sure don't look old enough t'have been to the Trench, man. Uncut night was my favorite—cheap beer and lots of hot sleazy guys. Man, we'd get so stoned…"

Tim shook his head at the word *stoned* and put the matches back in his pocket. He stepped through black curtains and waited for his eyes to adjust. He saw threads of red Christmas lights across the ceiling. He worked his way past pool players and found a stool at the corner of the bar. Candle wax dripped everywhere. Tim wondered why someone didn't clean it up.

Loud music enveloped him. It beat the traffic noise outside and the thwapping sound of the helicopter that reminded him of a police sweep. He no longer pictured the mirrored ball... or was it only hiding in some corner of his mind? Tim concentrated on breathing, *be-ing*, and he tried to act normal, even though he sensed that normal didn't matter much here. The bartender appeared, hairy and shirtless with a crooked smile. "...getcha, stud?" was all Tim could make out. He wanted to come down a little, but he wasn't sure which direction that was... where *he* was. It had to be somewhere in San Francisco. He had never been this stoned in Minneapolis.

"Screwdriver," Tim said. "Please." He never drank screwdrivers, but orange juice sounded healthy, even though the drink was mostly vodka. He felt for his pocket and had another moment of panic. He'd lost the hundred-dollar bill. Hell, he couldn't even find the pocket. It had to be there... not the one with the matches. Yes, now he found it.

The bartender reached under a drawer to make change. Tim put $90 back in his pocket and pushed the rest of the money across the bar. It was a good tip, but he thought of the old saying: *what goes around comes around.* Tim's own tips had been generous today and it was easier to leave it all than it was to count. The bartender grinned and clanged a dinner bell. Tim hated that noise. "Buy you a drink, Trench boy?" It was the man who had borrowed the matches outside.

"Thanks, no, I got one," Tim said.

"How about a shot, then?" he asked. "Tequila? Jaeger?"

"No thanks… I'm fine, really." Tim looked down and the man wasn't wearing pants. Tim was sure the man had pants on when they were outside, but now he was sitting on his pants, which were draped across his barstool. He wore shoes with Velcro straps and he was stroking himself with one hand while he held his beer in the other. That was all the man had on—a black leather jacket and tennis shoes with Velcro straps.

Tim blinked and got to his feet. "No thanks," he said again to the half-naked man. He asked the bartender, "What's the name of this bar, anyway?"

"This place is called the 'Hole in the Wall,' hon," the bartender said.

"Thanks," Tim said and walked toward the faded daylight streaking in through dirty front windows. He found a seat on the bench beside the pool table. A handsome man of about forty-five was shooting pool very poorly with a fat boy who wasn't much better at it. Now Tim remembered that he'd been here once with Jason, but it was late at night. His eyes didn't need to adjust that time. They had parked Jason's car right in front, but Tim wasn't paying attention to where they were. He thought he remembered this place being further south in the Mission district. He and Jason had gone to El Rio earlier and stopped for a drink at Esta Noche, but Jason was driving. Tim never would have found the Hole in the Wall again except by accident.

He didn't want to think about Jason now. He didn't want to be here, either. He finished his screwdriver and returned the empty glass to the bar. As someone who worked in a restaurant, Tim couldn't leave an empty glass for someone to have to pick up later. He should use the toilet before he left. He didn't want to be arrested for indecent exposure between parked cars on Folsom Street in broad daylight. He entered a doorway and found the narrow room with a trough. Tim closed his eyes as he opened his fly, heard the sound as piss hit porcelain and he felt the pressure ease. He was a skydiver in freefall, nowhere near ready to pull the chute until the last drops slowed to a stop. This was almost better than sex. "Man, you must have been holding that for hours!" It was the Velcro-shoe man beside him, still with no pants. Tim spun around and headed out. He was still buttoning his fly as he reached sunlight.

It was much too bright, but Tim was relieved to be outside. He walked a block up Folsom Street and turned left toward Harrison. There was someplace he planned to go today, but he couldn't remember it now. It must not have been important. That's how things usually worked. If there was something important he would be doing it, not wandering around as stoned as this.

Then that sound returned, but Tim couldn't see the helicopter. He was on the patio of the Lone Star Saloon and he didn't remember how he got here. He was glad to see Mavis, the Tarot card reader in her usual spot and many large men who took up twice the space he did. Tim held a bottle of beer in his hand and raised it to his lips. Cigar smoke choked him and the cold beer soothed his throat.

Then the air was filled with sparkling light. Tim thought silver glitter was falling from the sky. Conversations stopped and the mirror ball lowered. It eclipsed the sky above the Lone Star's patio. It hovered and spun, dazzled and fanned the crowd before it lifted up again and moved on. The biplane was an after-climax and the sign was too close to read it anyway. Men went back to their talk and their drinks and their smokes. Tim heard a deep laugh and then a loud voice saying something about a party, but now he remembered he was on his way to the Eagle. He just didn't know why.

Corey... that was the boy's name. It all started coming back, but Tim was in no shape for some kind of sexual performance,

even for money. He'd entertained the idea earlier, but now
he was too stoned. Besides, the kid wasn't his type. He was
cute and Tim was flattered, but there were plenty of guys in
town who would screw for money. Tim hardly felt qualified
to compete with the pros. Still, if the poor kid expected him
to show up, Tim could at least buy him a birthday drink with
some of that hundred dollar tip from his rich Uncle Fred.

Where was his cap? Tim saw his reflection in the window
of a truck on Harrison Street. The intensity of his stoned state
was abating, but he wished he had his cap. He must have
dropped it when he was with the old lady. He shook his head.
It was too late to go back there now. The Eagle was in sight.

Like many places in San Francisco, the Eagle Tavern
reminded Tim of Jason. Tim knew better than to dwell on
the past, but if he hadn't known Jason was at work at Arts
right now, Tim wouldn't have gone near the Eagle. He would
have avoided the Lone Star too, for fear of seeing Jason with
another guy.

There had been lots of guys before Jason, but most of them
were just sex. The only other one who really affected him was
David Anderson back in High School and he was Tim's first.
When Tim started seeing Jason the contrast between the two of
them finally appeared as vast as it was. In High School he and
the coach were always sneaking around and sometimes the
danger of getting caught seemed like part of the excitement
for Dave. With Jason, on the other hand, it felt like they were
showing off. Between Dave and Tim there had been a mutual
need. Between Jason and Tim there was desire and a sense of
sex being downright fun.

Tim remembered how it felt to ride around in the
convertible and pull up outside a bar with Jason. Swarthy
bikers would get off their machines like cowboys climbing
down off their horses, legs spread so wide they might be just
learning to walk. Even the butchest ones would turn to look

at Jason in his red Thunderbird with the top down. And they would look at Tim too, of course. On the rare occasions when the two of them had a night off together to go dancing, other guys on the dance floor stepped back to make room. It was as if there was a spotlight on the two of them when they were together.

Now that Tim was alone he felt invisible. It wasn't a lack of confidence. He liked himself. He wasn't afraid to look in the mirror on the worst mornings. The difference was… people noticed *them* when he was with Jason. People wanted to see who the lucky guy was that Jason had chosen. They wondered what Tim had that they lacked. They wanted to imagine themselves in Tim's shoes. No, when he really thought about it Tim had to admit that what they wanted was to find a way into Jason's pants.

Tim worked his way across the Eagle patio. People were lining up for a buffet, but as stoned as he was, the smell of sauerkraut didn't appeal to Tim's munchies. Some of the hotdogs on the grill were charred and shriveled. Some had broken. They reminded Tim that he should pick up condoms before heading home.

Now, he had both pot and condoms on his mental tally of things that were running low on Collingwood Street. He should find a pen and start a list, but some things you just remember. If groceries popped into his head, cream and coffee or bread and butter, English muffins and strawberry jam, those he would have to write down. Tim always forgot the basics. He could use the last coffee filter and not remember until the following morning with a hangover. The kitchen floor was always cold under his bare feet as he folded a paper towel to fit the basket of his Mr. Coffee machine. The supermarket and Walgreens were just down the street, but he would have to put on clothes to go there.

Tim remembered where he was now and worked his way across the patio. The bartender there gave him a big smile like he recognized Tim. Maybe he was a customer at Arts or… "Where's Jason?" the bartender asked. "I'm surprised he dares to let you out of his sight, Hot Stuff!"

It was just as Tim feared. He hadn't been to the Eagle in a month or two, but it was always with Jason. "He's working tonight at Arts," Tim answered. "How about a Heineken?"

"Sure… that first one's on me." The bartender set the beer in front of Tim with a wink. "So you're out on your own, huh?"

Tim smiled and winked back, reaching into the pocket of his jeans for a dollar bill, but he had to change a bigger bill to leave a tip. He tried to cross the line of men waiting for the outdoor trough and he got jostled by some drunks. One of them scowled and whined, "Hey, the line starts back there!" Tim ignored him and kept on walking.

"Hey, stud!" Someone else tugged at Tim's sleeve. It was one of those four guys from brunch. He was taller than Tim remembered. "It's about time you got here. Frederick almost gave up on you and hired someone else for Corey's birthday present."

Tim looked down at his elbow until the man let go of him. It was a move he'd seen Jason make in this kind of situation. "I'm not in the business…" Tim raised his glare from his elbow to look the guy straight in the eye, "… of being told what to do." The man shrunk back and Tim let a smile come to one corner of his mouth. If he couldn't be with Jason, maybe he could act like him, although Jason would have taken the guy up on his offer of getting paid to be a birthday present. Jason wasn't a hustler either, but he'd make sure the kid got his money's worth and Jason would enjoy the adventure. Tim was almost stoned enough to do it, too. The tightness around his head was gone. The edginess had evaporated, but his mind and body were fluid enough to still play this game. "Where is the birthday boy?" Tim asked.

"They're inside. We were shooting pool, but it was too busy. The lines for the toilet got in the way of our shots. I came out here to use this one, but it's almost as crowded. At least there's some fresh air. It smells like someone dropped a bottle of poppers by the pool table."

"They probably did." Tim smiled. Jason would be friendlier now that he had the upper hand. "My name is Tim Snow. I don't think I caught yours."

"Donald," the man said. "My partner is Jerry. We... um... do business with Frederick. Corey is his nephew."

"Seeya, Donald." Tim stepped back a moment and then let the crowd's next wave of motion carry him across the Eagle patio toward the side door. If he was going to play the part, he needed more ammunition. Tim stepped up to the main bar and held up a crisp twenty. He'd also learned from Jason how to get a busy bartender's attention without making a sound. "Do you have any chilled vodka?"

"Just Stoly."

"Great! I'll have a double shot and another Heineken." A beer bottle at his hip would look good. If he smoked, this would be the time to light up, but he was in California, anyway. The laws were so strict these days you could hardly smoke outdoors. Tim reached the wide steps at the back of the bar in time to see Corey slouched over the pool table. Frederick was shaking his finger in the boy's blank face. The other man named Jerry leaned into Corey's chest like a linebacker and hoisted him over one shoulder. He carried the dead weight down the stairs over the heads of the crowd and out the door.

Tim saw an open bar stool and sat down to finish his beer. "So much for my new career in hustling," he laughed to himself, "and so much for my becoming just like Jason."

Tim looked up at the TV and wondered why it wasn't showing pornography, but the thought only reminded him of how stoned he was. This was a bar, not a sex club. There was a game on, but nobody was watching. A deodorant commercial showed two guys in a shower scene and then wearing towels in a locker room. The guy on the bar stool next to Tim smelled like he needed a shower too. It was time to head back toward the Castro.

Tim walked up Harrison Street toward the Lone Star, thinking he might go look for his cap at the place where that woman was staying with her brother. The address must be on the invitation she gave him, but he couldn't find that either. Damn, it was his favorite baseball cap, too. Tim turned left on 11th Street but he didn't see Clementina. Maybe it didn't run this far south. He kept walking all the way to Market Street and it seemed like hours had passed. One of the old Italian streetcars pulled to the stop at Van Ness. Tim was a runner in high school, but right now his feet were lead weights in leather boots. The light changed long before Tim got to the corner and the streetcar clanged off toward Castro Street and the end of the line.

He zipped his jacket up to his neck and stumbled toward the stairs in front of the stony fortress of the Bank of America. Tim wanted to be home or at least back in his own neighborhood, but he would wait underground away from the wind. The helicopter was still out there somewhere. Tim imagined he could hear it beyond the wisps of fog that scurried past him. Soon that cool white blanket would be pulled down from Twin Peaks across the jagged skyline of steeples and streetlamps to tuck the whole city into bed for the night.

Chapter 4

Underground, the crowd pressed onto the K-Ingleside car. Some people must have been waiting a long time. Tim wedged into a spot at the end of the car and grabbed for a place to hold on between the jeweled fingers of a middle-aged lady and the glove of a shorter man reading a Chinese newspaper. Tim noticed a girl who looked familiar. She sat beside a boy who fondled her earlobe with chubby fingers. His hairy arm was slung around her shoulder and he was pierced in so many places he reminded Tim of his co-worker Jake. Tattoos snaked between his knuckles and Tim wondered how he would ever find a job or make himself presentable on his wedding day, but it was the girl Tim really noticed.

"Beth," Tim said under his breath. The doors closed and the streetcar jerked to a start. Passengers swore and apologized for stepped-on toes. Tim held on tight and stared at the girl. He only had two stops to go—Church and Castro. It wasn't Beth, but she was about the same age Beth had been when they first met. Tim smiled and wondered what had become of his old friend. The girl on the streetcar had a scar from the corner of her mouth to her left ear. She didn't look much like Beth except for the scar. Beth had straight black hair. This girl's was curly blonde with purple streaks. It might be black naturally, but Tim didn't think so. Besides, this girl wasn't old enough to order a drink and Beth was closer to Tim's age, nearing thirty by now.

The scar didn't show very much while the girl listened to her boyfriend whisper in her ear. It was when she talked that her face formed a crease around it. When she laughed, her face became disfigured in a way that no amount of make-up could help, but at the same time her laughter made her beautiful. She was exactly like Beth.

Tim met Beth in high school after he moved in with his Aunt Ruth and Uncle Dan. He had to go to a different school than the one where all hell broke loose with the track coach. Beth had recently transferred to Edina from Chicago, so they were both new. She lived with her paternal grandmother after her mother's boyfriend scarred Beth's face in an attempted rape.

Tim didn't have any physical flaws, but Beth recognized that he was scarred, too. The two friends felt familiar to each other right away. Tim's scars weren't apparent to anyone else except his Aunt Ruth who knew his whole story. Tim wanted to put his arms around this girl on the subway and tell her that everything would work out okay, but he just stared. Even though he was stoned he knew it was rude to stare but he couldn't help it.

Tim remembered the tree house. That's where he took his friend Beth. It was overgrown with vines by that time. Uncle Dan had built it for Tim's cousin Dianne, but she was already in college. Tim and Beth would climb up there and smoke grass and let their feet dangle. They looked over the fence at the neighbors' pool and listened to his Aunt Ruth's ancient 8-track tapes of Neil Young or Nancy Wilson, depending on their mood.

Beth had good grass by high school standards. The first time Tim got high was in that tree house. She won his trust enough to find out why he was living with these relatives instead of his parents and she told him some of her story too, but Beth found his more interesting.

"I had a crush on him," Tim remembered telling her. "My grades weren't great, but I could run fast. If I wanted to get into college, it would have to be on a track and field scholarship. Besides, the coach made me feel good about myself in ways my parents never did." Tim took another hit off the joint at that point, but Beth didn't interrupt. When he was slow to start in again, she asked the coach's name.

"Dave... David Anderson. There must be a hundred guys in Minnesota named Dave Anderson, but anyway..." Tim handed the joint back to her. "We were at a track meet in Duluth. I twisted my ankle and he took me to a doctor and gave me a ride back to Minneapolis in his car instead of going back on the bus with the team. He had car trouble, so we stopped to eat and then he found out it would take a lot longer to fix than he thought. At least that's what he told me."

This was the point in the story when Tim's voice always faded off, not that he told it often. He didn't even think about it much anymore. The hardest time came months later in front of the school board, that panel of men his father's age, men in dark suits whose thumbs fondled their wedding bands as Tim answered questions. They agreed that Tim must be to blame. Dave Anderson was a church-going man with a beautiful wife and a perfect little daughter. He might have a drinking problem, but there was help for that. Tim Snow must have instigated this distasteful business that went on.

Beth never pressed Tim, but she didn't discourage him. "Dave and I stayed in a motel that night. He bought us some beer that we drank in front of the TV. He talked about pretending I was his kid brother or something; I don't remember. He could always talk me into anything. Anyway, that was our first time—my first time with anyone." Beth lifted the joint to her lips to relight it. It was easy to tell her about Dave because she didn't judge. She accepted the way things were, including the scar on her face. Or maybe it was because they were so stoned, just as stoned as he was today, years later on the crowded subway under Market Street.

Tim stared at the girl and remembered telling Beth, "It wasn't just sex. Dave took me fishing sometimes. My parents thought that was a great idea. My dad never had time to do things like that. Dave knows some great spots out in the woods where there aren't any people for miles around. He tried to get me interested in photography, too. He took lots of pictures of me, of the two of us sometimes. I wish I knew what happened to them. He even knew how to develop them himself in his basement, but I always had other things on my mind when we were in the darkroom."

Beth just let out a low whistle at that point and Tim grew quiet. He didn't tell Beth about the time he got a cramp in his leg and tried to stand up too quickly. He nearly knocked over a tray of chemicals, but Dave held his hand on the top of Tim's head and pushed him back down. He wasn't finished yet.

"Then we started getting careless around school. I'd run an extra lap or two after the rest of the team hit the showers. They'd be on their way home, but Dave was waiting for me. It seemed almost natural to find him soaping up in the shower room and he'd wash my back. He was right out of college, not that much older than me. When we finally got caught we were parked in front of my parents' house. My mother was standing in the dark behind the curtains in the living room window and she watched me give him a simple innocent kiss goodnight. After all we got away with up until then, we got busted for a kiss!"

Tim still remembered that kiss. It was the last time he would kiss a man for a long long time. The coach went back to his wife and took a different job in a different school district. Tim went to live with his Aunt Ruth and Uncle Dan to finish high school in the suburbs where nobody knew him, either.

"Who you staring at, faggot?" The voice of the tattooed boy on the subway made Tim jump.

He didn't mean to stare at the girl. She must get more than her share of stares. The boy stood up to meet him face to face and fear crawled up Tim's back like the blade of a knife caressing his spine.

It was his own fault. He was stupid to make the girl uncomfortable and he deserved whatever came next. He braced for a blow, but he still kept on looking at the girl and he meant no harm. Thoughts of Jason flooded back to him. If Tim could muster up Jason's attitude at the Eagle he could... "Castro Station... K-Ingleside... Outbound." The crackle of a recorded voice broke the spell.

Tim sidestepped the boy and leaned in close to the girl with the scarred face. "Is your name Beth?"

"No, my name is Amy... Do I know you?"

"I guess not," Tim admitted. "You reminded me of a good friend I haven't seen in a long time and it's really nice to see you again. I mean her. It's really nice to see *her* again, even though I know you aren't her. It's nice to be reminded of her. I didn't mean to bother you... I'm sorry..."

"That's all right." The girl named Amy smiled the way Beth smiled. Her face became homely and beautiful at the same time. Tim wanted to touch her and hug her, but the doors were open and a crush of bodies piled off the streetcar. The boyfriend stood behind him staring at Tim like he must be insane.

"This is my stop. My name is Tim and it's nice to meet you, Amy. Take care of yourself…"

"You too, Tim." She shook his hand and Tim wanted to kiss her cheek on the side away from the scar, but he stepped off the streetcar just before the doors closed behind him. When he looked back at them the boy had sat down again with his arm around Beth's shoulder but she was Amy now.

The outdoor escalator was broken, as usual. People trudged up the stairs from Harvey Milk Plaza to Castro Street. By the time he got to the stairs they were empty and Tim bounded up them two at a time.

The fog swirled around him and Tim realized that no one in San Francisco knew his story. Everyone on Castro Street must have a story of his own and Tim's past would pale in comparison to some of them. There would always be people in the Castro who had to come even farther than he did to seek the freedom they'd always dreamed of and escape the nightmares of their pasts.

Chapter 5

Tim didn't spend a lot of time at Arts outside of working hours. The restaurant was around the corner from Tim's apartment and his bosses were also his landlords, so he saw them nearly every day. They'd invested in real estate before the Castro became trendy, gay and expensive. Since Jason and Tim were no longer sexually involved, that was one more reason to avoid the place. Tim wanted to get beyond all that and since he had to walk up that block on his way home, he thought he might as well stop by the restaurant. He barely set foot inside the door when he regretted his decision. Artie was in one of his moods.

"Don't even think about asking for next Saturday off," he started in before Tim had a chance to sit down. The place was quiet and Jason was nowhere in sight. "I don't care if it's the party of the century. You can go there afterward but I need you to work first. I'm sure it will last 'til dawn. I told Arturo we should just close for that one night, but he won't hear of it. He's convinced that some of our regulars will come in. You and I might be the only ones here, Tim. I already told Jake and Patrick that they could go. Don't give me any grief! They asked first. Jason is going, too, but he's tending bar at the party. He'll make a lot more in tips than he would here, that's for sure."

"What party?" Tim felt out of the loop. Artie wasn't exactly the go-to person to find out what was happening around town. Ever since Finocchio's closed, Artie's life revolved around Arturo and the restaurant. He had gained at least thirty pounds and retired his old act along with a wardrobe of feather boas and sequined gowns that no longer fit him.

"*What party*? Where the heck have you been? You don't mean to tell me you missed that noisy helicopter flying around town all afternoon with the giant disco ball dangling from underneath it …"

"Oh, that," Tim said. "Yeah I saw it, but I didn't know what it was all about. I was South of Market when it came through there."

"We had customers from Marin County said it was clear up over Stinson Beach this morning. It hovered over the intersection of 18th and Castro for the longest time, just spinning away, with that little airplane dragging a banner making great big circles in the sky. You should have seen the crowds on the sidewalks. Everyone ran out of the restaurant. They didn't even care that their drinks were melting. I haven't seen anything like it since the total eclipse. You'd have thought it was the Martians landing in a UFO or the second coming of Judy Garland!"

"It hovered over the patio of the Lone Star, but I couldn't read the banner. I don't have plans for Saturday night, Artie. It's fine by me if you need me to work. Where is this party, anyway? I don't know anything about it."

"It's at the Moscone Center. Everybody's talking about it. I guess those reunions at the Trocadero have been so successful it gave them the idea to go big-time. I'm sure most of the kids your age will be there. I'm way too old for that sort of thing, but even with Jason out, I shouldn't have any trouble handling the bar by myself. Nobody will be on Castro Street, you can mark my words."

"It seems pretty quiet in here tonight, too. Where is everybody?"

"Viv asked to leave early. Her new boyfriend came by to pick her up. Maybe this will be husband number five. Or is it six? I can't keep track. It must be serious, though. You know Viv. She'll plunk out show tunes on the piano until we turn out the lights as long as there's one lonely drunk still throwing tips in the brandy snifter. Tonight she didn't have a single request during the last hour she was here."

"Where is Jason? It's early for him to be off, isn't it?" Tim had been trying to act like Jason earlier and he thought he would like to see him now, if only for a minute.

"I let him and Jake leave after the dinner rush. I think they were heading down to the Lone Star, too. I'm surprised you didn't run into them. Patrick is still here. He must be in the kitchen. He and I can handle the stragglers. That couple of lovebirds down the bar are just having after-dinner drinks. Hey, what happened to the birthday boy? I thought you had a hot date lined up. You were supposed to meet him at the Eagle, weren't you?"

"I went to the Eagle after a stop at the Lone Star and earlier I went to this other place called the Hole in the Wall. Have you heard of it?"

"No, but I haven't been South of Market in years," Artie answered. "Don't change the subject. What happened to that cute young boy with the FBI man?"

"The birthday boy... Corey... he won't remember much about this birthday, I'm afraid. He's going to wish he didn't remember the hangover he'll have when he wakes up tomorrow. They had to carry him out of the Eagle by the time I got there."

"Pity." Artie wiped his wet hands with a bar towel. "Do you want a drink, Tim?"

"No thanks, Artie. I'm on my way home."

"Come on, Tim. Let me buy you one," Artie insisted. "It's been so slow in here tonight; I'm about to go crazy from boredom. Keep me company. I made a fresh pot of coffee… how about an Irish?"

"Oh okay, Artie. Twist my arm…"

"Tell me about your day after you left work," Artie prompted. He wasn't the fastest bartender in the world, but he knew from experience that most people liked to talk about themselves. "Was it busy down there South of Market?" He placed a steaming mug in front of Tim and slid a layer of fresh whipped cream across the top, then stuck a plastic straw inside it.

"I guess so." Tim stirred until the layer of whipped cream turned his drink one color. "Yeah, come to think of it, it was. The Eagle was packed. They had a benefit going on. The Lone Star was pretty busy, too. The weirdest part was that I was so stoned! I still am a little, I guess."

"You and your pot! I haven't touched that stuff since Vietnam."

"It wasn't even my pot," Tim protested. "I met this old lady named Vanessa on the streetcar and she got me stoned. Vanessa Caen, no relation to Herb Caen, she said. She doesn't even live here." Tim remembered the joints in his pocket and pulled them out along with the party invitation and a napkin they were wrapped in.

"You were smoking pot on the streetcar with an old lady?" Artie asked.

"No, not *on* the streetcar. I helped her carry her groceries back to her brother's apartment and we got stoned there. You should see the place. It's like a big loft on Clementina Street or is it Clementina Alley...? I don't know." Tim unfolded the paper and the joints fell out. "The address must be in here somewhere."

"Tim, put that away before someone sees!" Artie scolded.

"Nobody's looking, Artie. Don't be so paranoid. I'm invited to a party there and I'm curious enough that I might go. Hey, when did you say that party is happening at the Moscone Center? Saturday? That's the same night as this party, I think." Tim unfolded the invitation, rewrapped the joints in a paper napkin and slid them back into his pocket. "That's strange..."

"What is?"

"It doesn't say when the party is. It just says Harley Wagner with the address on Clementina and a phone number to RSVP, but no date or day or time. I think I left my baseball cap there, so I'll call and see."

"This weekend is that other big hoopla in town, too," Artie said. "That big *Men's Revival* is going on down at the Civic Auditorium. It starts on Friday night and lasts all weekend."

"What's that, another gay party on the same night?"

"No, it's nothing like that; in fact, it's just the opposite. That evangelist from Minnesota is coming to town. Remember the 'Promise Keepers' a few years back? Maybe you're too young. They tried to teach men to take back their macho roles in society. It was sort of a backlash against the feminists. This guy is as homophobic as he is sexist, though. He's anti-abortion, anti-women's lib, pro-war, but his biggest cause is getting the gay rights laws repealed... all in the name of Jesus, of course."

"The only evangelist from Minnesota that I've ever heard of is Billy Graham," Tim said. "But I thought he was dead, or at least retired. Maybe he has a son."

"No, Tim, it's at the Bill Graham Auditorium," Artie tried to explain. "Bill Graham was the rock promoter who died in a helicopter crash, but that was years ago. Maybe that's what you were thinking. You don't read the papers, do you Tim?"

"Sure I do. I get the Chronicle delivered. I always read the *Datebook*, at least. Bill Graham and Billy Graham were two different people. I'm almost sure of it."

"Look at today's paper, Tim." Artie pulled the news section out from behind the bar and opened it to page two. Here it is: *Arlo Montgomery to hold weekend prayer vigil at Civic Center.* There's a picture of him in Chicago last weekend. It says he drew a crowd of over 50,000."

"Imagine the lines at the men's room," Tim said, laughing.

"Imagine the *action* in the men's room," Artie chuckled. "With 50,000 guys on their knees for an entire weekend, there must have been something going on besides prayer. It sounds a little like the army and I can tell you from my own experience…"

"Wait a minute," Tim said. "Let me see that picture. That guy behind the preacher… I know him!"

"Who?" Artie asked.

"That's my old track coach from high school. That's just got to be him. I'm sure it is!"

"Were you in track, Tim? I never heard about that part of your life. You were a high school athlete? How sexy!"

"It's a long story," Tim said, sipping at his Irish coffee again. It had cooled off enough to drink it now and he finished it in two gulps.

"I'd love to hear the story in detail when you have a chance sometime."

"Aw… not tonight, Artie. I wonder if I have this paper at home. I couldn't have thrown it out. I didn't even look at it yet."

"You can have this one."

"Thanks, Artie," Tim said as he stood up and slipped his arms into his leather jacket. "I gotta run. And thanks for the drink."

"Sure, don't mention it." Artie took the coffee mug and wiped down the bar.

As Tim stepped out onto Castro Street he thought he heard a helicopter's rotors spinning somewhere in the dark, but this time it was only his imagination.

Inside his apartment Tim peeled off his jacket and headed straight for the kitchen. The Sunday Chronicle was still in its plastic wrapper with a free sample of laundry detergent inside. Tim spread it onto the kitchen table and sat down to untie his boots. His feet were sore from so much walking today. He didn't go South of Market very often and almost always got a ride with Jason in the past.

Tim didn't think it had to do with any of his elusive psychic *powers*, but he sensed that people were playing tricks on him today. The old lady named Vanessa reminded him of his grandmother at first, but once they got stoned he didn't think so. The girl on the subway reminded him of Beth, but this girl named Amy was only a teenager. Artie couldn't have known about Dave Anderson, either. Even if he did, he couldn't have doctored a photograph in the newspaper and there was no reason for Artie to mess with Tim's head.

He was paranoid; that was all. He pulled the joints out of his pocket again and placed them on the kitchen table. He crumpled up the paper napkin they were wrapped in and tossed it over his shoulder. It hit the trashcan in the corner and Tim thought how much sexier basketball would have been than track and field, but Tim barely cleared 5'9" on a good day. He eyed the joints, but he pushed them away and opened the Sunday paper. There was the picture of Dave Anderson behind this preacher who was raising such a fuss.

Tim read the caption again, "Arlo Montgomery..." He had never heard of the man, but he didn't follow much news about evangelists. He felt sheltered from their anti-gay hatred in San Francisco. Even if he didn't live up to his potential, even if he never developed the "gift" he'd inherited from his grandmother and had never asked for, even if Tim's life was as ethereal as the fog and he was lost forever in a land of pure fantasy, at least he felt safe here.

Arlo Montgomery didn't matter to Tim, but David Anderson might. There was something Tim wanted to remember about his first time with a man, even though he wanted to erase everything that happened later. Tim stared at the grainy black and white picture in the newspaper and shook his head. He picked up one of the joints and his lighter, but he thought better of it and set them back down.

Dave Anderson still looked good. Tim had no doubt this was the same person. He would be in his late thirties by now. Tim stood and stretched his legs in his stocking feet, adjusting his crotch to make more room in his tight Levis. He remembered checking into a motel off the freeway—a teenaged Tim and the man who was his mentor and his coach and his first lover.

Tim thought of all those times in the locker room after the rest of the team went home. The smells of sweat and chlorine still turned him on to this day. Maybe he had called it a night too early. Sunday evenings at the Edge could be fun and it was just down the street. Nah... he was in for the night and he might as well get out of these clothes altogether.

The fog had chilled him to the bone and a hot soak sounded like a good idea. Tim put the plug in the tub and turned on the faucet, but someone else in the building must have had the same idea. The water came at less than full force, but at least it was hot. Tim got undressed and thought back on all that happened during that year he turned sixteen. The fights with his parents were the worst. He could still feel the shame brought on by his father's anger and his mother's tears, but he also remembered that she did nothing to help. The last time he saw her was with one eye swollen shut from his father's fist. It was ten o'clock in the morning, but she had a glass of bourbon in one hand and a soggy handkerchief in the other. Tim walked away with a duffel bag full of clothes and he never looked back.

The picture in the San Francisco Chronicle brought a flood of both good and bad memories. If his Aunt Ruth hadn't picked him up that day, Tim might have come to San Francisco sooner. That would have been okay, but he was glad he finished high school instead of ending up like the teen-age runaways he saw on Polk Street. He didn't envy any of them.

While the bathtub filled, Tim walked back to the kitchen, looked at the picture in the Chronicle again and rubbed his eyes. He opened the door onto his tiny patio. It seemed even colder outside than when he came home, but he was naked now. He thought he heard the helicopter again, but it wouldn't make sense to pull an advertising banner behind an airplane in the dark. Tim shut the door again and pushed the deadbolt lock. As he slid under the steamy water he realized the sound was only the bathroom fan.

Tim hadn't had one of his dreams in a long time. He'd had them since he was a boy and he still hated to admit how much truth they had in them. This time he was on Alcatraz riding a Ferris wheel. Jason's voice beside him said, "Great party, huh?" It felt natural to be with Jason again. They were still a couple and Jason's hand was on his knee, but when Tim turned toward him to respond, the hand belonged to his old track coach. Tim allowed Dave Anderson to hold his hand and they stared out at the lights of ferryboats lined up across the bay. Each one dropped off hundreds of party-goers and then headed back toward the city for more.

It was a warm starry night without a whisper of fog. The enormous mirror ball they had watched flying over the city all week was now suspended from a crane above the dance floor where the old prison cellblock used to be. Tim looked down at a sea of flesh of thousands of bare-chested men. He could smell their sweat.

Tim watched the orange ball of sun settle into the gray Pacific beneath the towers of the Golden Gate Bridge. He pointed and said to Dave, "Look at the sunset. Even without any clouds, the sky is full of colors." Then Tim turned toward the person beside him and David Anderson became the naked man from the Hole in the Wall. He wasn't looking at the sunset, but staring at Tim, sliding one hand up Tim's leg and stroking himself with the other.

The Ferris wheel became a roller coaster that ran all the way around the island. Tim heard the music from the dance floor even louder than the rattle of the tracks. He could hear screams as they started their steep descent toward the cold black water of the bay. Vanessa Caen was in the car ahead with a tall, thin man. Tim thought this must be Harley, as sick as he was. Tim knew he was dreaming, but this was one of his *real* dreams.

Amy and her tattooed boyfriend were in the car behind him. The boy had one fleshy arm around her shoulder and his other hand played with a silver switchblade knife. Tim faced forward again and the thin man—Harley—held a gun now. He pointed it straight up beside his right ear where Vanessa couldn't see it.

Then the roller coaster plunged and left the track. It spiraled down and down into the icy waters of San Francisco Bay. Tim swallowed and sputtered and spat soapy water as he lifted his head from the bathtub. He had slid all the way under and the water was cold now. He pulled the plug and turned the shower knob up as hot as he could stand it. The pressure was back at full force and it beat against Tim's goose-bump flesh until it warmed him again. He wrapped himself in his biggest towel and went to bed.

Chapter 6

Tim slept late Monday morning. When he shuffled down the hallway to make coffee he noticed the two fat joints on the kitchen table where he'd left them. *Killer weed* was the only way to describe it. That old lady Vanessa must be used to the stuff. Tim was no lightweight either, but this was more potent than anything he'd smoked in a long time. Tim kept his pot in a ceramic dog on a shelf in the living room, but he stashed these joints in a Band-Aid box in the medicine cabinet. He didn't want to get them mixed up. Vanessa had said it was medicinal and if Harley was her much younger brother, Tim figured Harley might be a long-term AIDS survivor.

Tim pulled on his jockey shorts to go grab the morning paper from the front steps. He heard the clank of the gate and footsteps in the hallway and wondered if he should put on some pants. It was probably Teresa from the third floor or Ben and Jane Larson from the second. Arturo and Artie wouldn't be awake before noon on a Monday morning after

they worked Sunday night. The other apartment upstairs was
rented to a new guy named Malcolm, but Tim hadn't met him
yet. He heard a thud against the door and opened it a crack.
"Tim, is that you?" A voice asked.

"Teresa! Yes, it's me. Who else would it be? What are you
doing?" He pushed his door open farther and realized the
thud was his newspaper hitting the threshold.

"I thought I'd pick up your paper when I got mine. You
startled me."

"Then I guess we're even... sorry," Tim said. "How are
you doing?"

"Not so hot, to tell you the truth. I had a terrible night.
There aren't any decent heterosexual guys left in this town
and I'm leery ever since my divorce about meeting anyone
who isn't as straight as an arrow, you know..."

Artie and Arturo had told Tim about Teresa's marriage
travails. Her high-school sweetheart Lenny, whom she'd
married in college, met another man shortly after they moved
to San Francisco. "It's really none of my business, Teresa, but
thanks for the paper. I had sort of a rough night myself."

"Come upstairs and tell me about it, Tim," Teresa said.
"I'll make us a pitcher of Margaritas... or would you prefer a
Bloody Mary?"

"Teresa, I haven't even had coffee, yet."

"Oh, my! I hope you don't think... I mean... I don't want
you to get the wrong idea, Tim. I have nothing against gay
guys and I hope you don't think I was coming on to you, of
all people..."

That was not what Tim thought, but he didn't know how
to extricate himself from this conversation. Now he felt guilty
about being so abrupt with her. "I didn't think that, Teresa,
but you do know that I'm gay, right?"

"Aren't all the cute guys in this city gay, especially in the
Castro?"

"Maybe I could come up later, okay? I really need some coffee and I wanna take a look at the morning paper and there's an important phone call I have to make."

"Come up anytime, Tim. I'd love to swap stories about our awful evenings last night, but I won't force you. My door is always open and I make a mean Margarita! You're not working today, are you?"

"Not until this evening at the earliest. Artie didn't have the schedule finished last time I checked. Maybe later…" he repeated, "honest."

The Chronicle had another article on an inside page about the evangelist Arlo Montgomery. He had been attracting throngs of followers as well as large groups of gay-rights activists protesting his appearances. This weekend in Madison Square Garden a capacity crowd paid to get inside while a couple of hundred demonstrators were arrested outside. Tim wondered what would happen in San Francisco. The Sylvester birthday reunion was planned for the Moscone Center the same weekend that the biggest enemy of gay rights since Fred Phelps would be only a few blocks away. It couldn't be mere coincidence, could it? From now on he would watch for news of Dave Anderson and Arlo Montgomery, but Tim felt almost relieved that he had to work on Saturday night so he wouldn't have to choose between the party and the protest.

He flipped through the local channels on the TV in the kitchen, but it was too late for anything but soap operas and game shows. He turned to the jazz station and Diana Krall's voiced oozed out. Tim poured a cup of coffee and carried the paper out to the patio. The fog had burned back far enough that it might be a warm day in the Castro. This might be a good day for housework and his geraniums could use a good soak, but they could wait another day.

He turned again to the article about Arlo Montgomery in New York. It continued on the back page with another small photograph of the preacher alongside a larger picture of demonstrators in handcuffs. There was no sign of Dave Anderson and no mention of the upcoming event in San Francisco until the last paragraph. Today was only Monday. Tim wondered whether the helicopter would be out again this afternoon or if that sort of advertising was only for weekends. Tim reached for the phone and punched in the number of the restaurant.

Arturo's nephew Jorge answered in Spanish. Jorge helped Arturo in the kitchen and seemed like a decent kid, but the language barrier got in the way. Tim only wanted to get his schedule and was curious about whether he was working with Jason. Being so stoned on Sunday afternoon and trying to act like Jason, Tim thought there was enough of a switch in his attitude that it might be time for him and Jason to become friends. Tim gave up on Jorge's English and told him he'd call back later. He wanted his cap back, so he picked up the invitation to the party on Clementina and punched in that phone number.

"Hello! Harley Wagner residence! Vanessa Caen speaking!" Her voice was so loud that Tim moved the phone away from his ear. "Hello? Hello?"

"Hello," Tim shouted back, wondering if the woman had gone deaf overnight. Then he heard music in the background and realized it was more of Diana Krall, the same jazz station he had on.

"Just a minute, please," Vanessa shouted. "Let me turn down this music… Oh, I don't know where the knobs are… hold on, please!"

Tim took another sip off his coffee. When she returned and repeated her hello, Tim responded, "Hi, Mrs. Caen. This is Tim Snow. I was calling to ask if you ran across my baseball cap. I think I dropped it there yesterday. It's black and it has the word 'colt' across the front in gold letters."

"Timothy! How nice to hear your voice! Why, yes, indeed... your chapeau spent the night outdoors on the deck, I'm afraid. The gardener found it on the floor this morning near where you and I were sitting. Are you coming to the party? You could pick it up then."

"That's another thing, I might have to work that night so I thought I'd pick it up before then, maybe even this afternoon if it's convenient, but when is the party? The invitation has the name, address and phone number, but there's no time or date."

"Oh, how silly of me," Vanessa said. "I must have given you one of the bad ones. Here we are living above a print shop and the first batch of invitations came out without the date on them. Isn't that funny? It would be lovely to see you this afternoon though, Timothy. You can meet Harley if he's up and about. I'm sure he'd love to meet you. He's lying down right now, but he ate a fair amount of breakfast this morning..."

"And the party?" Tim tried to ask.

"Yes, of course if you have to work, that's a shame, but you could come by afterward, couldn't you? Harley's friends are a late bunch. They might go on all night."

"Yes, but when?"

"Oh, you can come over any time for your hat, my dear boy. I'm not going out at all today. I'm just puttering around here, writing a few postcards. I'll look forward to seeing you this afternoon, then. B-bye."

Tim thought it might be nice to have a visit with his neighbor Teresa after all. At least Teresa made better sense than Vanessa Caen and he never knew when having a friend in the building might come in handy.

"I'm so glad you decided to join me, Tim. I needed a hair of the dog and I hate to drink alone." Teresa mixed Bloody

Marys in a heavy ceramic pitcher at her kitchen sink. "You grab a couple of those glasses and let's take these babies out on the deck, huh?"

Tim noticed how sunny Teresa's apartment was compared to his own, which sometimes felt like a cellar on gloomy days. The hardwood floors were bleached oak and there were shiny wood tables and chairs, bookshelves and molding. The sun sparkled off the rich grain and everything was spotless. For someone who liked to start out Monday mornings with a stiff drink, Teresa must be fastidious about housework. It made Tim feel guilty about leaving his apartment downstairs in such a state.

"To happy days and good neighbors, Tim," Teresa raised her glass.

Tim lifted his and smiled. "I'll drink to that. What a great view of the Castro Theatre! I'm jealous."

"Don't tell me this is your first time up here. I can't believe it!"

"It's my first time up here in daylight. I stopped by at your Christmas party last year, don't you remember?"

"I'd forgotten you came to that fiasco, Tim. My God, that party was the single biggest disaster of my newly-single life! Don't remind me."

"It wasn't your fault the power went out. It was out all over town. It was lucky you had so many candles. I ended up having a good night... I took home that cute guy who was here all by himself. I think his name was Eli."

"Eli? I had no idea!" she said. "We work together. Half the female teachers at school are after him, but he's so shy I wondered if he was gay. Why didn't you tell me this before?"

"He's gay all right, but that's history," Tim said. "He was a lot of fun in the sack, but way too closeted outside of it. He was only in my apartment for an hour and then he wanted me to promise not to say anything to you about it. I hardly knew you, so it wasn't as if he needed to worry. I forgot all about him until right now. But you still haven't told me about last night, Teresa. What happened? Ooooh… good Bloody Mary."

"Thanks, Tim. It was Lenny's recipe. The secret is fresh horseradish… most people use too much Tabasco for the heat… and plenty of good vodka, of course. That was one advantage of marrying a gay guy. I learned enough entertaining tips to give Martha Stewart a run for her money. I'm sorry, Tim. I didn't mean to offend…"

"What's offensive? I'm not that close to Martha. She never calls me anymore."

"You know what I mean, silly… the gay thing."

"No offense taken, Teresa," Tim smiled and tried to put her at ease. She seemed to be wound up this morning. No wonder she drank. "But don't change the subject. You haven't told me what happened last night?"

"You're the guest, Tim. You should get to complain first."

"My night was no big deal. I was supposed to meet up with this kid and help him celebrate his birthday South of Market, but I got there too late." Tim left out the part about being offered money. He didn't know his neighbor well enough. "And I hate spending Sunday nights alone, especially when there's nothing on TV. Then I had some wild dreams when I got home, that's all. What happened to you?"

"I went out with a couple of girlfriends from school. We started at some clubs in the Mission… you know how it goes. A guy might send over a round of drinks, but then he'll go for one of the skinny ones, not me. It's a bitch to be in a room full of guys and not a single one of them is interested. I guess you wouldn't know, as cute as you are, Tim. I might as well have been in a gay bar!"

"You'd be surprised, Teresa, I know exactly how it feels to be in a room full of guys and not a single one is interested... even in a gay bar."

"Last night was different, though. I guess this guy was looking for someone with a little more meat on her bones and *yours truly* fit the bill."

"Yeah? Then what happened?"

"We danced. We had a few more drinks. We came back here. I should have suspected by the way he was slurring that he wouldn't be able to..."

"Get it up?" Tim finished her sentence.

"I was going to use a gentler term like 'perform,' but you got the idea. Even that wouldn't have been so bad if he'd been able to do anything else, but he was too wasted. I was afraid he was going to pass out on me, so I suggested that he go and take a shower to sober up."

"That must have been about the time I was having a bath. The water pressure in this building is terrible, isn't it?"

"You can say that again," she agreed. "This was fairly early in the evening, considering we'd been to about five bars. Anyway... he came back from the shower raring to go, but he only took a minute..."

"Oh, no..." Tim sympathized.

"Oh, yes...and then he passed out. He was so cute this morning, though. He really wanted to make it up to me, but he had to go to work. He was out with some buddies last night, but he lost track of them so I drove him back to Oakland this morning and I just got home."

"You're not planning to see him again, are you?"

"Why not? He can't get any worse. Besides, he likes me. He's taking me out next Friday. Another Bloody Mary, Tim?"

"No thanks, Teresa." Tim felt his bare wrist but he'd left his watch downstairs on the dresser. "What time is it anyway? I'm not used to starting out my Monday mornings like this.

It's lucky you're a teacher and you have the summer off, but I've got to check the schedule at work and then go down to Clementina to get my cap back. Thanks for the drink, Teresa. We'll talk later, okay?"

Tim also wanted to stop at home to e-mail his Aunt Ruth. He had several questions to ask her about Dave Anderson. Then he tried the restaurant and caught Arturo in the office. "Yes, Artie's got you down for Wednesday through Saturday nights and then Sunday Brunch again," Arturo told him over the phone. "You're not on tonight or tomorrow, though. How does that sound?"

"Fine, Arturo, thanks..." Tim said. He was sure that Artie wasn't working tonight either, after pulling a double on Sunday, which meant that Jason was scheduled for Tim's nights off.

"Artie mentioned that you stopped by last night, Tim. I guess he didn't do the schedule until after he closed, though. How was the rest of your Sunday after you left work?" Arturo asked.

"It was okay, I guess," Tim said. "Arturo, could I ask you something personal?"

"Sure, Tim... shoot!"

"Do you remember what it was like to be single in San Francisco?"

Arturo laughed. "Not really, Tim. It was a long time ago and it seems like Artie and I have been together since we were kids. We met in Viet Nam, you know..."

"Yeah, I've heard that, but not much about it."

"There's not that much to tell, kid. We messed around during the war and then we really hooked up again about a year later. May I give you some advice, Tim?"

"Sure!"

"Maybe you need to find a hobby you enjoy... besides *men*, I mean..." Tim could hear Arturo open and close a cabinet in the background. "Do you like to read? I have some good books you could borrow. I'll sort through them one of these days and find a few that might be right up your alley. Have you ever thought about a drawing class? You're a sensitive guy."

"Paint-by-numbers were the only drawings I could do, Arturo. I took an art class in high school, but I never felt confident. At least with paint-by-numbers, I knew when they were finished."

"I know, Tim," replied Arturo. "There're lots of things in life you never know when they're finished. Speaking of which, I hope you're not still pining over Jason."

"I'll be all right, Arturo… Thanks." Tim knew that both of his bosses wanted the best for him, but Jason was one of their employees, too.

When Tim stepped outside onto Collingwood Street the air felt heavy. The light had a crystalline quality that made him want to turn down a dimmer switch on the day. Distant buildings faded into silhouette with the sun behind them. On his short walk to Market Street the Castro neighborhood felt almost European, a small Alpine village tucked away in a high mountain pass. Tim loved looking up from the corner in front of the Twin Peaks bar past the giant rainbow flag as the last tendrils of morning fog burned back over the hills.

The streetcar driver clanged her bell to let people know she was leaving. It was a red and yellow bullet car and the driver was the same lady who had let him ride free one recent day when he forgot his wallet. No matter what else happened, Tim was glad to be in San Francisco.

The driver smiled when Tim flashed his pass, but continued her conversation with a couple of elderly tourists in the front seat. "Mission Dolores is at 16th Street. This one's 17th and when I turn the corner we'll be heading down Market toward the Ferry Building. If you don't mind walking, you could get off at 16th and Sanchez and it's due east. Otherwise, you can stay on this car to Church Street and transfer to a #22 Fillmore bus and get off when it takes the left turn at 16th and the church is right across the street on the next corner."

Tim had heard it all a thousand times. Her job wasn't all that different from his. Bartenders, waiters, cab drivers and friendly locals were always giving directions in this town. It was high season for tourists, probably sweltering where they'd come from, but shivering in San Francisco in the shorts and T-shirts they'd brought with them. Tim wore shorts and a tank-top today, but he had a hooded sweatshirt tied around his waist and he intended to be back in the Castro long before the fog made its return around four o'clock.

"Will you join us for a bite of lunch?" Vanessa Caen was dressed all in green today. She handed Tim a joint as soon as he stepped off the elevator. "We're having shrimp salad in heirloom tomatoes from the farmer's market with toasted baguettes and a nice bottle of California chardonnay."

"You sound like me announcing the specials at work," Tim said. "Did I tell you I was a waiter? I guess I can hardly refuse after that description. I am a little hungry."

"Good! Here's your hat. Wait outside on the deck and I'll go get Harley," she beamed. Tim adjusted his COLT baseball cap to shade his face from the sun. It was warmer today than the last time he was here and the fog had burned back to expose the Sutro tower. Vanessa had left the joint with him, but he was careful this time. He took two shallow tokes and didn't hold them long.

"Hello there, Timothy Snow." A deep voice came from behind the philodendrons. Tim jumped up to shake hands with the man in the wheelchair being pushed by his much smaller sister.

"How do you do, Mister Wagner."

"Please—call me Harley, Tim. Vanessa told me that a handsome young guest was coming by for his hat, but her description didn't do you justice. I'm glad you've agreed to stay for lunch."

"I didn't intend to stay. I only came by for cap, but…"

"That grass is good, isn't it?" Harley said. "I'm afraid I wouldn't have an appetite without it. Let's move to the table, shall we?" Vanessa had already gone inside, but Harley wheeled himself beyond a redwood planter where a glass-topped table was set for three. The rooftop deck was larger than Tim's apartment.

"Have you lived here long?" Tim asked.

"Long enough," Harley answered. "Since the 60's, but let me hear about you. Vanessa just told me you were kind enough to help her with the groceries yesterday. Did you find your friends afterward?"

"I was… too late." Tim didn't feel like talking about Corey and those people he hardly knew. "It was dark by the time I got home last night. I stopped at the bar down the street first, the Hole in the Wall, and there was a naked guy in there.

Harley laughed and said, "They used to be known for that. In this part of town, you never know what kind of excitement you'll find."

"I guess you've seen a lot of changes since the 60's."

"Oh, yes…" he said. "The Castro was just a working-class family neighborhood then and most of the gay bars were on Polk Street or in the Tenderloin. Folsom Street was hardly what it became. Of course, that's nothing today like it used to be, either, before AIDS. What kind of work do you do, Tim?"

"I'm a waiter at Arts on Castro Street," Tim answered. "Do you know it? It's been there a while. The owners are Arturo and Artie. They're also my landlords. Arturo was a chef before they bought the restaurant and Artie used to be an entertainer at Finocchio's."

"Artie Glamóur? Vanessa!" Harley shouted. "Tim knows Artie Glamóur! Where are you, sis?"

"I'm coming!" Vanessa appeared pushing a cart full of wine and food. "Did you say Artie Glamóur? I remember him! She was almost as big as Charles Pierce in his day." Vanessa seemed comfortable mixing pronouns.

"Where did you see Artie?" Tim asked. "Did you really see him perform? I've never even seen Artie in drag."

"At Finocchio's, of course," said Vanessa. "We used to go there in the seventies, after I retired."

"Vanessa was in show business, too. She was in the original Broadway cast of *Finian's Rainbow*," Harley bragged as his sister set their salads in front of them. Harley reached for the wine and corkscrew and then offered it to Tim. "Perhaps you'd be so kind as to open this, Tim. We don't often have a professional in our midst."

Vanessa said, "All I ever wanted was to be a Rockette, but I was at least four inches too short."

"Four inches can make a world of difference, can't they, Tim?" Harley said with a wink. Tim tried not to laugh, but Vanessa was clueless.

"I was also in the touring company of Oklahoma. That was fun, but I got tired of living out of a suitcase. Harley saw me dance at the Orpheum Theatre. I had a big part in the dream ballet sequence. My brother was a wonderful dancer too, weren't you, Harley?"

"Never on the stage. I loved dancing at Dreamland and the Music Hall on Larkin Street was one of my favorite discos. You're too young to remember them, I suppose." He tapped his index finger on his glass as if he heard some faraway music.

"I've heard people talk about the Trocadero," Tim said. "There's a big dance party this weekend at the Moscone

Center. You must have heard the helicopter yesterday, Mr. Wagner… Harley."

"Yes, it woke me from my nap. Are you going?" Harley asked. "We're having a party here this weekend too, but I won't be dancing, I'm afraid."

"I have to work Saturday night," Tim said, "but I could go later, maybe. When is your party?"

"I remember the old dance parties like *Night Flight*," Harley said. "There was one on Mission Street back in 1980s called *Snow Blind* and I'm sure we all *were*. Those were the days when everyone was all coked up or on acid or MDA."

Vanessa shouted, "MDA—Mary, don't ask!" and erupted into laughter.

Harley continued. "There was a big party called *Stars* and everyone had to buy their tickets in advance and send in a photograph. All night long the partygoers' faces were projected on the walls above the dance floor, so everyone was a star that night."

"Sounds like fun…" Tim said. "There's also that other thing going on this weekend… that religious revival or whatever they call it. It sounds like a one-man anti-gay crusade and it's just a few blocks away. I was thinking about going down to join the protesters." Tim *had* thought about going there, but more out of curiosity to see if he could spot his old coach than out of any sincere political motivation.

"Are the boys from Act-Up organizing a riot against the Christians?" Harley asked.

"I don't know who is organizing things," Tim said. "I'm sure it will be in the gay papers on Thursday or there will be posters all over the light poles in the Castro."

"I wish I could go," said Harley. "I haven't been to a good riot since the night of the Dan White verdict when we trashed city hall and burned police cars."

"Were you there?" Tim's eyes lit up.

"You bet!" Harley beamed. "I'd be hard pressed to decide nowadays between rioting and dancing all night, though." He looked down at his legs in the wheelchair and pushed back from the table as he reached for another joint. "Who am I kidding? I'd go dancing all night if I could. Screw those crazy bigots. Give me a disco ball and Sylvester's music any day!"

Chapter 7

Tim awoke Tuesday morning to a moment of panic. He couldn't remember what he'd done the night before. More joints had followed the lunch on Clementina Street and then he'd been tempted to look for Jason, but didn't. He remembered stopping at the Badlands for a beer and then at the Edge, where they were playing Country music. Some guys recognized him as their waiter at Arts and sent over a double shot of premium tequila. That was what caused this hangover. If he'd stuck with beer, it might not have been so bad.

He pulled on a pair of shorts, made coffee and sat down at his computer. When he touched the mouse the screen sprang to life and Tim remembered his intoxicated prowling when he got home last night. There was more Spam than usual this morning—offers for Viagra and Vicodin from Canada or videos of underage Asian girls peeing, all for one easy credit card payment. No thanks. Tim hoped he hadn't made any on-line dates that he'd forgotten about. Half a dozen guys had viewed his profile on dudesurfer.com and left him offers between 2am and 5am. He imagined they were sleeping by now or still tweaking. No thanks again. He almost deleted the one e-mail he was looking for:

Dear Tim—

How lovely to hear from my favorite nephew! You sound well, but what a lot of questions you have. I'll do my best to answer them. First off, I'm fine, though it's been muggy and the mosquitoes are worse than ever this year. There's a big controversy about spraying chemicals near the playground, understandably, but the mosquitoes are as big as my hat and the little ones come in from a day of hopscotch just covered in nasty bites.

You asked about Beth and you know, Tim, as often as I've thought of her, I don't know much. You might try a search on the Internet. My girlfriend Deirdre had some luck with that when she was looking for an old "friend" after her divorce. It turned out he was still married, though. You knew Beth had plastic surgery, didn't you? Maybe not... It's been so long. I've heard you can barely see her scar now and she married a cello player from the Minnesota Orchestra, but he's not with them anymore. They trade some of those musicians around like they were athletes or something. He's with the Boston Pops now, if I'm not mistaken. The last time I saw the symphony was in Powderhorn Park for the Fourth of July, like we did when you and Dianne were kids, remember? I didn't recognize anyone, but they probably put in substitute players for an event like that when it's outdoors and free. I always tried to get Dan to buy season tickets to the symphony, but it was all I could do to drag him to the Guthrie for a play now and then. He never missed a Vikings game though, no matter how poorly they played... so much for culture.

I saw an article in the St. Paul Pioneer Press about Arlo Montgomery, but there weren't any pictures. Now Tim, I know it's none of my business, but I don't like the sound of you dredging up ancient history. If David Anderson is involved with something like that Arlo Montgomery anti-gay business, it's all the more reason not to get mixed up with him again. There must be lots of nice boys in San Francisco and I couldn't ask Nancy even if we were on speaking terms. What would I say? "I heard your closeted husband left you again to join some religious crusade against gay people?"

I did happen to see Nancy, though. She didn't see me. I saw a darling sundress in the Marshall Field's ad, so I drove over to Southdale. I could have gone on-line to order it, but I was invited to a garden party at the Carlsons' that weekend and it seemed just the thing. Well, wouldn't you know, the Southdale store was out of them, but I ran into Bebe Halverson and she said they had just what I wanted at Bloomingdale's at the Mall of America, only better, in more colors and even cheaper than the sale price at Marshall Fields. I hate to deal with all that traffic, but I didn't have a thing to wear and as I said, it's been so muggy that I wanted something cool and fresh. By the time I got over there, the air conditioning in my car was acting up and I was fit to be tied. I found just the dress I wanted, though, in turquoise with white piping and I already had the perfect sandals.

I decided to treat myself to a glass of wine and there I was at the Napa Valley Grille and thinking of you out there in California, but I'm sure the food is better in the real

Napa Valley than here in the suburbs. Anyway, I looked up and there she was behind the counter—Nancy Anderson! She was working there! I was so surprised I nearly choked on my Chablis. I don't think she saw me because the next thing I knew she took off her apron and left. It was probably time for her break, I guess, unless the sight of me made her walk off the job!

The Carlsons asked how you were and I didn't know what to tell them, but now I will. I've got to call and thank them, anyway. They had a good turnout, terrific food and best of all Dan wasn't invited, so I didn't have to worry about any messy scenes with him and that girl who is young enough to be his daughter. The only sour note was when—do you remember their old dog, Maxie? Yes, she's still alive—must be a hundred and ten in dog years. Anyway, she knocked the lid off the ice chest that was full of walleye filets and hot dogs for the grill. The poor old beast ate half of them before anyone noticed and then she got sick in the pool. Fortunately, she was down by the diving board and the kids were in the shallow end. There were plenty of other things to eat, so we weren't in danger of starving. I prefer my walleye fried in a nice beer batter anyway, but I suppose grilling it is a lot healthier.

I almost forgot to tell you I ran into Paula Nelson at the Carlsons' party and she'd seen Nancy, too. Remember Paula? She was the Spanish teacher at the high school where Dave was before you transferred over here, so of course she knew him and I mentioned that I'd seen Nancy. Well, Paula says Nancy told her that she and Dave are going through a trial separation while he goes off to get "born again." Nancy said she told Paula, "I was born Lutheran and I still am and being born once ought to be enough for Lutherans if you take to it properly the first time."

Between you and me, Tim, she had a hard time of it when their daughter was born by C-section, so maybe all that talk about birth just isn't her cup of tea.

I would love to come and visit sometime. Thanks for asking. Are you sure you have room for me? I could get a hotel. I haven't been to San Francisco in ages, but September was always a nice time of year. After school starts the tourist season settles down a bit and things aren't quite as crowded, but the weather is still good. I remember those lines for the cable car at Powell and Market! When I was at Stanford, we used to drive in for an afternoon and walk down Haight Street or go to Golden Gate Park and pretend we were flower children, too. What happy times those were!

Now I want you to promise me you're staying safe if you know what I mean and I think you do. I'm sure you're happier in San Francisco than you would be here, but that doesn't mean you aren't missed and loved. I'll look at flights for September and it'll be here before you know it. Keep in touch, Tim, and if you see Dave Anderson, be careful of your heart. I'd hate to see you get hurt again.

Much love always,

Aunt Ruth

Tim was excited at the prospect of seeing his Aunt Ruth again and he knew the guys at Arts would get a kick out of her. He scanned the remaining e-mail. His HIV meds were ready to pick up at Walgreens—Tim dreaded sharing that news with his Aunt Ruth—and his credit card bill was available for viewing. That made it sound like a body at a wake. He was about to stand up from his desk when a new message came in about protests being planned against Arlo Montgomery this weekend. Tim glanced at the grainy pictures on dudesurfer. com once again. Lots of guys were looking for sex on a Tuesday morning. Tim wasn't sure what he was looking for, but it was too nice a day to waste it indoors.

Tim poured a mug of coffee and stood barefoot outside the back door in his tiny garden. He considered what Arturo had said about a hobby—besides men—and told himself again that his affair with Jason was part of the past. He also thought about his Aunt Ruth's upcoming visit and her concerns about Dave, Tim's old track coach. Part of him wanted to scream, "Everybody just leave me alone!" but he also knew that people's concerns were out of love.

Here he was in sunny California on a Tuesday morning with nothing to do. The local news said there was a mild off-shore breeze and the paper showed the lowest tide at the Golden Gate Bridge at 1pm. If he had a car he'd love to drive to San Gregorio or Devil's slide. He could take the bus to Baker Beach, but it would be crawling with straight people on such a warm day. Tim didn't want to immerse himself so deeply into the Coppertone world of horny heterosexuals.

Then he remembered Land's End. Jason had taken him there once. Tim showered and shaved and stuck a paperback book inside his beach towel. Maybe he could space out enough to get into reading while he basked in the sand. On impulse he also tossed the joints in the Band-Aid box into his backpack as he headed out to catch the #24 Divisadero bus to Geary. He bought a sandwich at the Honey-Baked Ham store and found a seat all the way in back of the #38 Geary to Point Lobos. Tim flipped through the Chronicle, but saw nothing today about the evangelists coming to purge his sins.

Tim walked north through the smells of eucalyptus and didn't see another soul until he reached the sign: *Caution — People have been swept from the rocks and drowned.* He peeled off his T-shirt as a woman jogged around the bend and smiled at him. At the bottom of the hillside a half dozen men were already in the clearings between rocks and driftwood. Tim groped through his backpack for a bathing suit and changed. He liked being naked, but he loved a tan line. Jason had once told him that the white stripe made a perfect target in the dark.

Tim didn't see anyone he recognized at the beach, but he eyed a couple of guys he might like to know. He reached for the Band-Aid box and took one hit off a joint. Jason had told him about a time when this beach was a playground for gay men, when dozens or hundreds dotted the primitive landscape on any sunny day with their naked tanned flesh among the ancient boulders. Every open space of sand boasted a figure who might have been an Olympic athlete. The rocks were the bases of statues of living Greek Gods. That was before they built the stairs making the beach accessible to anyone and everyone. That must have been before AIDS had come along, too.

Tim took another hit off the joint. He'd heard people claim they saw things on drugs. He didn't want to see things and he didn't like drugs, only pot. His grandmother had seen things and he had supposedly inherited her gift. Every once in a while it crept into the back of his mind like a guilty conscience, but he hardly noticed it lately except in his dreams.

He liked pot. It helped him stay in the present. He could stare at a painting in the DeYoung Museum for an hour and imagine what went through the artist's mind as he chose each brush stroke. Tim could also stare at his big toe for an hour, but at least he wasn't having visions about what might happen, nor was he dwelling on the past. He looked at his watch and an hour had passed. This shit was strong! He took his watch off. He didn't need a tan line there.

"Tim, is that you?" came a voice from the distance. Tim glanced up at a group of men coming toward him. The voice sounded familiar. It was Jake from work and those guys from Sunday—Corey, the birthday boy, and that guy who'd carried him out of the Eagle and the other one. What were their names?

"Hey, Jake!" Tim waved. So much for solitude. "What's up?"

"Look who I ran into on the street. You remember Corey, don't you?" Jake asked. "And Donald and Jerry?"

"Hi guys. How much longer are you in town? Where's the other one... Uncle Fred?"

"He went to L.A. to take care of some business," Jerry said. "We're heading back to Denver tomorrow morning, but we stopped on Castro Street to shop and ran into Jake there, who was nice enough to drive us out to the beach."

Tim guessed the limo must have only been at Uncle Fred's disposal or maybe it was a special treat for Corey's birthday.

"I borrowed my roommate's car," Jake explained as he undressed, revealing pierced nipples and navel, plus a new tattoo on his left side that Tim had never seen before. "This would have been a great day for San Gregorio, but I have to work tonight, unlike *some* people I know. Do you mind if we join you?" Jake had already spread a blanket beside Tim, so the question was a mere formality.

"Sure, why not? How do you like San Francisco, Corey? Did you have a good birthday?" Tim couldn't resist asking the poor kid about it.

"I don't remember much after we left the restaurant. I must have passed out. I'm glad I got to see you again today."

Tim told himself he wasn't interested in younger guys, but he had to admit this kid was really something. Corey unbuttoned his shirt to reveal a body that wasn't overly developed, but got Tim's attention. When Corey slipped out of his jeans to reveal a pale blue Spandex bathing suit, Tim's mouth watered. He pictured Corey's long athletic legs in a jock strap. "It's nice to see you again, too... your last night in town, huh? Have you got big plans?"

"Not yet," said Donald from the blanket a few feet away. "Any suggestions?"

Before Tim could answer, he heard a helicopter and expected to see the gigantic mirror ball come into view, but it was only a news crew headed toward the Golden Gate Bridge. "It's too bad you won't be here for the party on Saturday night," Tim said. "You must have seen the helicopter and the biplane out on Sunday, or was that too late for you?"

"We saw it," Jerry said.

"We saw it from the limousine on Sunday morning before we came to the restaurant," Corey said. "They told me it was out again later, too. Are you going to the big dance party, Tim?"

"I have to work... alone," Tim said for Jake's benefit. "That way my co-workers can go. Besides, there's going to be a demonstration at the Civic Center this weekend and I thought that might be more interesting."

"I'm going to the protest at the airport when Arlo Montgomery's flight comes in," Jake said. "I can still make it to work on Friday and go to the party on Saturday, but I'll feel that I've done my gay duty."

"Is there always so much happening in San Francisco?" Corey asked, wide-eyed. "I think I should live here."

Jake said, "You wouldn't be the first guy to visit San Francisco and fall in love... with the city, I mean."

"Anybody like to share a joint with me?" Tim asked and reached for his lighter. There was no way he wanted to talk about falling in love. This was his day to escape. "It's some killer weed I got from an old lady I met on MUNI."

"Are you serious?" Jake asked.

"None for me," Donald said. "The rest of you go ahead."

"Yeah, I met this old lady and helped her with her groceries. She's visiting her ailing gay brother and I had lunch with them yesterday because I left my cap there on Sunday. Great apartment," Tim said as he relit the joint. "The kitchen was like something out of *Auntie Mame*, but with wonderful views and an enormous deck where he grows this pot... or the gardener does."

"He has a gardener for an apartment?" Jerry asked.

"Well... someone to come and water the plants," Tim explained. "It's not like it's a full-time job or anything. The brother is in a wheelchair and he has permission from his doctor to have a few plants, but I'm warning you it's really strong stuff. A little goes a long way."

"Where did you come from, Tim?" asked Corey as Jake handed him the joint. "Are you a native San Franciscan?"

"Minneapolis," Tim said. "South Minneapolis and then Edina—the suburbs."

"Nice lakes," Corey said and took a deep hit, holding it as long as he could and handing the joint to Tim.

"Thanks," Tim said. "Your legs are nice, too... What? Did you say lakes? Oh, shit! I'm already pretty stoned."

Corey started to laugh and cough at the same time. Tim jumped up to pat him on the back. "Are you all right? I've got water in my backpack. Here, I'll get it for you."

"Thanks, Tim," Corey said, taking a sip. "I was in Minneapolis last summer and I had a great time. Hey, where does that trail go?"

"Did you say this was your first trip to San Francisco, Corey?" asked Jake.

"Yeah."

"That trail goes up to some paths where boys like you could get in big trouble," said Tim.

"Sounds like fun. Do you want to show me?"

Tim grinned. "It can be treacherous. You should put your sneakers back on. Come on... "

They were close enough to the water at low tide that waves crashed above their knees and then slithered back down between the boulders. Corey stared off toward the Marin County headlands and watched a Norwegian freighter head out to sea as a spray of mist spread across his face. "Hey, Tim! Wait up! I think I must be more stoned than you are."

When Corey caught up Tim said, "I was gonna take you to the cave, but it looks like some bears beat us to it."

"Huh?"

"Bears... big hairy burly guys? You must have bears in... where are you from? Denver?"

"I live in D.C. now until I finish college next year. The three of us will fly to Denver tomorrow and then I'll go on alone from there."

"Who are those guys... your personal bodyguards?"

"Donald and Jerry are a couple. They've worked for my Uncle Fred since before my parents died. I was still in high school when he took me in."

"I'm sorry," Tim said.

"I was lucky in some ways," Corey went on. "They've always been around to look out for me. Families come in all different shapes and sizes, I guess. My Uncle Fred figured out I was gay before I did."

"I have an aunt like that," Tim said. "My Aunt Ruth took me in... and my Uncle Dan, but they're not together anymore. I was always closer to her than anyone else."

"Are your parents dead, too?" Corey asked, almost hopeful that they shared such a coincidence.

"Yes... no... I don't know," Tim said. "They might as well be. At least *I'm* dead, as far as *they're* concerned."

"I'm sorry," Corey said. They stopped when two naked blonde boys ran past them, snapping towels at each other and laughing in German. "Do your parents know you're in San Francisco?"

"Maybe..." Tim answered. "My Aunt Ruth keeps in touch with them. My mother is her only sister. It seems like if you're going to disappear, why not San Francisco? I've met people here with much worse stories than mine. Listen, could we talk about something else?"

"Sure, Tim... sorry."

Tim smiled and said, "No problem." They continued westward and didn't talk at all for a while. Tim stopped and pointed toward a cruise ship that was coming into the bay.

"Look how close it is, Tim," Corey said. "You could almost touch it! Hey, are those rainbow flags?"

"Woo-hoo!" Tim laughed and waved. "It's a gay cruise! Lock up the children! The bars in the Castro will be crowded tonight. I wonder if they're all coming to the party on Saturday. Come on, Corey. Let's climb up there and I'll show you those paths you asked about."

Corey started up the steep path, but slipped backward. Tim stopped his fall by catching Corey's right butt cheek in his hand. "Careful!" Tim shouted above the waves. "I don't want anything to happen to you out here. I can just see your uncle sending his hired goons after me. They'll want to kill me instead of pay me..." Tim stopped short. He doubted that Corey knew about his Uncle's offer to pay Tim for sex and there was no reason this beautiful boy should have to pay anyone, Tim thought. Corey hadn't seemed to hear anything over the roar of the surf and Tim was glad that his words were swept away on the wind.

Once they were on solid ground above the cliff, Tim took the lead again. He ducked under a branch and Corey followed him into a clearing in the shade. "Wow, it's a lot cooler up here. I can't even see the ocean anymore, but I still hear it."

"Yeah, I know." Tim raised his hands to Corey's chest and rolled the boy's nipples between his fingertips. Corey moaned and leaned forward as his lips parted and his tongue found Tim's teeth. They kissed long and hard in the shadows until they had to stop for air. Tim took a couple of deep breaths and grinned. He felt like a kid sharing his favorite game with a new playmate.

Corey breathed deeply, too, and let his hands slide down from Tim's chest to his crotch. "I've wanted to do this ever since you came through those swinging doors in that restaurant on Sunday and handed me a menu."

All Tim could say was, "Mmmm..."

A half hour later they sat at the edge of the cliff, looking out toward passing sailboats near the north tower of the Golden Gate Bridge. "What are you thinking?" Corey asked.

"That this is always the time when I wish I smoked cigarettes."

"That's just great!" Corey frowned. "I hoped you might be thinking how sorry you are that I have to leave tomorrow."

"Of course, that's the other thing, but you have tonight, don't you?"

"What do you have in mind, Tim?"

"Well, I'm not working. We could have dinner someplace. I don't care where—Chinatown? The Mission? North Beach? I could show you my apartment. It's nothing fancy, but it's in the Castro, just around the corner from Arts. Or do you already have some secret plans? I shouldn't assume anything. Maybe your uncle's hired goons have your last night in town all mapped out for you."

"They're not bad guys, Tim," Corey said. "They've gotten into the habit of being overly protective ever since I came to live with my uncle. I don't think I need that much protecting any more."

"Protect you... from what? People like me?" Tim was stoned enough to feel paranoid now. He couldn't understand why Uncle Fred would be willing to pay Tim one day and then send out his bodyguards to protect Corey from him a couple of days later. "I don't get it."

"It's no big deal, Tim. My uncle has always been protective, even back when my parents were alive. He came out in a time when being gay was very secretive and now he's paranoid because he's convinced that everyone's after his money."

"Maybe he shouldn't flaunt it so much," Tim said. "Did you grow up in Washington D.C.?"

"Partly, yeah, but Tim..." Corey's hand slid up Tim's leg as he leaned in to bite at his ear lobe.

"Yeah, but what?" Tim asked.

"There are some things you didn't much want to talk about, right?"

"Yeah..."

"I feel the same way, okay?" Corey said. "We only have about twenty-four hours. Let's not waste them on talk. Let's spend them having sex. Let's get my stuff from the hotel and then go to your apartment. Or we could spend the whole night right here at the beach. I don't care. I'd be happy."

Tim heard a familiar sound and looked up behind them at a helicopter coming into view over the VA Hospital. The enormous mirror ball spun slowly and it came so close that Tim and Corey could see the face of the pilot. Tim wondered if he intended to rinse it off in the Pacific Ocean. "Look at how close he is! I think that pilot is as crazy as you are," Tim said and leaned over to kiss Corey full on the lips.

"Thanks, Tim. I guess that's a yes." The helicopter waited for the bi-plane to catch up. Tim finally saw the banner as it rounded the bend toward the Cliff House.

Tim read, "Dance... celebrate... Moscone Center...They must plan to advertise to everyone on Ocean Beach before

they head back to fly over the gay neighborhoods again."
He thought to himself that Harley Wagner would love this
party.

"Who is Sylvester?" Corey asked.

"He used to live in San Francisco. He was a famous disco
singer and a drag queen too. I like his music, but if he was
before my time, he was way before yours. You know that song
'It's Raining Men... Hallelujah!'" Tim snapped his fingers and
tried to sing.

"I guess I've heard it."

"Well, that song was by The Weathergirls. They were two
great big black women, Martha Wash and Izora Rhodes, who
started out as Sylvester's back-up singers, only then they were
called 'Two Tons o' Fun!' Your uncle's goons might remember,
but they don't look like disco types." Tim wanted to explain
to Corey that he'd probably heard and danced to Sylvester's
music without knowing it, but Corey kissed him again.

"I didn't know you had a suite!" Tim shouted as he ran
to the window. "What a great view! Don't you want to sleep
here on your last night in San Francisco?"

"Whatever you want is fine with me, Tim," Corey said.
"I mean—this is already paid for, but I'd like to see your
apartment, too. You could still show me around the Castro,
right?"

"Sure, but I don't have any view except the houses across
Collingwood Street and my patio in the back off the kitchen,"
Tim said. "This place is amazing! I thought you just had an
ordinary hotel room. Where are Donald and Jerry staying?"

"They have connecting rooms down on the 25th floor. I
was supposed to use one of them if I brought someone back
with me so that they'd be right next-door, but I guess they
trust you. My uncle and I were staying up here together, but

he's already checked out and gone on to L.A. I'll see him in D.C. next week."

"But you said Donald and Jerry were going to Denver, right?"

"Yeah... so?"

"The hired goons trust you to fly back there alone? What happens when you get to D.C.?"

"I'll finish graduate school... Oh, you mean that. Uncle Fred will have a car meet me at the airport," Corey explained. "You should come and visit sometime. We could have fun."

"I can't imagine living like that." Tim sat down while he watched Corey toss a toothbrush into a leather bag. "What does your family do in the government?"

"What are you talking about... the government?"

"I thought you said..."

"I live in D.C. because I go to school there, but my family isn't with the government in Washington," Corey said.

"What's your last name?".

"Am I making you nervous, Tim?"

"Just tell me your last name."

"Donatelli. Uncle Fred's last name is Iverson. He's Swedish. My mother was his sister."

"I never heard of either name."

"I'm half Italian and half Swedish, okay? What's your last name, Tim?"

"Snow, but I still don't understand why he thinks there's so much danger around you..."

"There isn't. My Uncle has a lot of money, okay? Uncle Fred breeds race horses and he's a little eccentric. He was my mother's protective older brother and he didn't approve of his sister marrying my father. Then he never believed my parents' death in Paris was an accident and he transferred his fears for her onto me."

"Ooh... just like Princess Diana," Tim whispered.

Corey threw a pillow at him. "He loves me very much, that's all. Can we get out of here and change the subject, please?"

"First let me take a leak, okay? I've never used the bathroom in a suite before."

"Can I help?"

"Sure, kid," Tim said with a grin. "But you're too young to be that kinky, aren't you?"

They boarded a red vintage streetcar in front of the Virgin music store and sat in the wide rear seat where they could hold hands and act silly all the way down Market Street. Tim felt like it was his own first visit to San Francisco. He pointed out City Hall and other landmarks along the way. "There's the BLT Center on the corner!"

"The... *what*... center?" Corey asked.

"Oh, that's just what Jake calls it, the BLT Center, like a BLT sandwich. It's really called... let me think... LGBT, I think. Lesbian, gay, bisexual, transgendered... am I forgetting anyone?"

"I don't know." Corey looked dazed and Tim kissed him.

Within a few minutes they were on the sidewalk nearing the Castro Theatre where a huge crowd was gathered outside. "What's going on here?" Corey asked.

"I'm not sure." They had to walk out into the street to get past the cameramen. Tim pointed and said to Corey,"That's Jan Wahl. She's a local TV personality. Oh... and the other one is Dame Edna. He's supposedly a straight married guy from Australia, but he goes in drag as this character of a housewife turned megastar. The guys in the background are from the Gay Men's Chorus. I saw an ad in the B.A.R. about Dame Edna appearing with the chorus. They must be shooting a promo for it."

"Which one is the drag queen?" Corey asked.

"The tall one in the funny glasses," Tim replied. "The one in the hat is Jan Wahl. She's a real woman on Channel 4, very gay-friendly."

At the corner of 18th and Castro three men dressed as psychedelic nuns handed out flyers in front of the Bank of America. "There is so much going on here," Corey said. "Is it always like this?"

"Those are just the Sisters of Perpetual Indulgence. This is nothing. Today's only Tuesday. Weren't you out here on the street on Sunday?"

"Yeah, but we left the restaurant right after brunch and then we took the limousine straight down to that place called the Eagle."

They crossed Castro Street at 18th toward Harvey's on the corner. Tim was about to explain to Corey that the bar was named for Harvey Milk and begin another history lesson, but he stopped in the middle of the intersection and looked back. Tim could have sworn that he saw David Anderson out of the corner of his eye. It was only for a split second. Then the man ducked into a cab at the bus stop and it took off turning right down 18th Street. "What's wrong? Who are you looking at?" Corey asked.

"Nobody... it just looked like someone I used to know, but maybe not. Come on." The sidewalk traffic thinned as they walked south and Tim's fingers slid around the back of Corey's neck. They kissed again.

While Corey used the bathroom, Tim checked his e-mail. Someone had sent him a private message on dudesurfer. com, but that could wait. A bird in the hand was worth more than the slim possibility that a computer date would be as good as advertised. Tim read the profile anyway, out of habit. He logged off the web-site and found Corey in the kitchen studying the photographs on the refrigerator. One showed Tim in longer hair next to a black Mustang in front of a building with monumental pillars. Another shot of Tim in the same clothes showed him posing next to the statue of *The Thinker* by Rodin, but Corey had no idea where it was taken. One showed Tim with his arm around a handsome black man with Half Dome in the background. Corey recognized that spot from Ansel Adams' photographs of Yosemite. Corey laughed at Tim in Mickey Mouse ears in front of Sleeping Beauty's castle at Disneyland. "There you are," Tim said. "Are you getting hungry for dinner?"

"Sure, pretty soon," said Corey," but who's the lady with you in this picture, Tim?"

"That's my Aunt Ruth I was telling you about. That was taken at a picnic by Minnehaha Falls in Minneapolis back when I was in high school. Hey, there's one of me at a track meet."

"That's you?" Corey asked. "You're *so hot!*" Corey made the word "so," into three syllables and stretched out "hot" so that it lasted for two.

If Corey's youth didn't fit with Tim's usual taste in men, he had to admit that 'the kid,' as he thought of him, was adorable. "So, you think I was hot in high school, huh?"

"Well… I mean…Tim, you still are, but I never knew you were a jock, too. Hey, most of these recent pictures are with the same guy. He's really hot, too. Who is he?"

"That's Jason," Tim said. "He's a bartender at Arts. We work together."

"You guys look like more than just co-workers here. Woof!" Corey was eyeing a photograph of the two men arm-in-arm wearing swimsuits.

"That was taken up north of here at the Russian River shortly after Jason and I first met. We dated for a while."

"You sure have a lot of memories on your refrigerator. I don't have nearly as many pictures of myself."

"You will when you get to be my age," Tim said and as soon as the words left his mouth he realized how old he sounded. He laughed at himself and exaggerated the effect by adding, "Give yourself another decade or two. I have drawers full of albums of sepia prints in the bedroom."

"Sepia?"

"Never mind!"

"I'd like to see them sometime, especially the jock ones. I'd like to see Jason, too."

"Maybe later… he's working tonight, but I think it's time to make some new memories," Tim said. "You didn't answer my question. Are you hungry?

"Yeah, but dinner can wait. Which way is your bedroom?"

Chapter 8

Tim had his faults, but being late was not one of them, especially where his job was concerned. His Aunt Ruth might say, "Punctuality is built into our genetic make-up from generations of ancestors having to allow extra time for travel through the deep winter snows." If anyone asked Tim he would just say, "I'd rather be early than rushed."

So Artie was worried when Tim didn't show up at the usual time on Wednesday. Jake had set up all the tables in the dining room by himself and Artie already had a few customers at the bar. Arturo stepped out of the kitchen, wiped his hands on his apron and asked, "Where's Tim?"

"We don't know," Artie and Jake said in unison, as if they had it rehearsed.

Arturo looked for Tim's number on the employee list behind the bar and headed back to the kitchen where it was quieter to talk on the phone. Vivian had already started her first set at the piano, a rousing medley of hits by Burt Bacharach with a couple of old Beatles tunes thrown into the mix.

Jake started to tell Artie about seeing Tim at Land's End, but Artie got side-tracked when a couple rushed in for a quick drink before the movie started at the Castro Theatre. Artie turned back to Jake and asked, "Where were we...oh yes... go on... did Tim and Corey come back from the beach with you?"

"No, they came back to where we were sitting and they picked up their stuff, but Tim said not to wait for them. He wanted to take Corey to the Cliff House for a drink and he said they'd find their own way back on the #38 Geary bus. Donald and Jerry started to object, but Corey insisted that he was in good hands, so they eased off. Then Tim and Corey headed west into the sunset. Well, it was only about three in the afternoon, but it *was* kinda romantic. I haven't seen Tim smile so much in a long time."

"That was probably because he'd been smoking that stuff again," Artie scoffed.

Arturo returned from the kitchen. "There's no answer at Tim's apartment."

"I hope he's all right," Artie said. "Those cliffs are dangerous. People have drowned out there."

"He's probably on his way right now," Arturo said. "You're fretting like a mother hen."

"I'm sure the worst danger they were in was from sunburn," Jake added. "It was fun to see Tim having a good time. He's been moping around so much ever since he and Jason split up."

"I know only too well," Artie said. "Maybe I should call Patrick to come in and work Tim's section. I hate to bother him on his night off. He's busy planning a protest, I'm sure, but we have a lot of reservations for later. It's not like Tim to let me worry."

"Hiya, Artie. Where's Tim?" Artie looked up to see Teresa, his tenant from across the hall on Collingwood Street.

"I wish I knew, Teresa. When did you last see him?"

"Last I saw him he was up at my place on Monday morning for Bloody Marys on the deck. Artie, I'd like you to meet Tony. He lives in Oakland. Tony, these are my landlords, Artie behind the bar and the chef here is Arturo. They also own this joint."

The men shook hands and Artie asked, "Are you two here for dinner?"

Teresa smiled at her date and reached for his arm. "I guess we could be... whatcha say, honey?"

"Yup," he answered, obviously a man of few words.

Teresa turned back to Artie. "Tony and I were supposed to have a date this Friday, but he just couldn't wait that long to see me again, couldja hon? So he dropped by my apartment this afternoon. What a nice surprise, huh? I was just telling Tim about Tony the other day, so I was kind of hoping to introduce them and show Tony off."

"If you're not in any hurry, you might as well sit down at the bar and have a drink. Or you could take a table in Tim's section and wait," Arturo suggested. "I'm sure he'll be along any minute. He's never been late in all the time he's worked here. I just wish he would call. This is strange."

"Heck yeah, why don't we just wait at the bar and have a drink first, okay?" Teresa pulled Tony toward her and they straddled adjacent bar stools.

"Yup," said Tony. "Fine by me. Scotch... Dewar's... a double... no ice."

"I'll have a Gold Margarita on the rocks with extra salt, if you don't mind, Artie," said Teresa. "You know how I like them."

Artie smiled. Even though Tony didn't have much to say, Teresa was capable of filling in any gaps in their conversation.

"What sort of work do you do, Tony?" Arturo asked.

"Construction," he answered and swallowed half his scotch before Teresa's drink was ready.

"How interesting…" Arturo said.

"Hey, there's a cab out in front," Jake said. "Maybe that's Tim now."

They watched a dainty woman dressed all in purple step out on the far side. She tried to help the driver wrestle a wheelchair from the trunk as a tall gentleman climbed out of the back seat and waited on the sidewalk. Arturo said, "Well, that's not Tim. I'd better get back to the kitchen."

The lady pushed the man inside in his wheelchair and helped him up as they settled themselves onto bar stools near the front corner of the room. Before Artie could get to them, he heard the lady say, "Harley, that's got to be him! I just know it is!"

"May I help you?" Artie placed cocktail napkins in front of his new customers.

"Artie Glamóur! Is that you? It *is* you, isn't it?" the lady asked. "We're some of your biggest fans. I'm Vanessa Caen and this is my brother Harley Wagner. It's such a thrill to meet you in the flesh. We used to go to Finocchio's to see you every time I came into town."

Artie smiled and blushed, but quickly protested, "No, no… I retired her years ago. It's just plain Artie now, I'm afraid. The wigs are in storage and the gowns are all in mothballs."

"What a shame," said the man named Harley. "You were such a hit. We came here to see Tim, too. This *is* where he works, isn't it?"

"Yes, but he seems to be missing at the moment. We're starting to get a little worried… Oh, look!" A black stretch

limousine pulled up in front of the restaurant and Tim
climbed out of the back seat before the chauffer could come
around to open his door. They watched Tim wave and mouth
his thanks.

"I don't believe it!" Jake said. "He must be moonlighting
at another job these days. This should be good."

Tim grinned when he saw that everyone was staring at
him. "Hi, guys! Hiya, Harley... Vanessa. What a surprise to
see you two here! Hey Artie, I'm sorry I'm late. There was
an accident on 101 coming back from the airport. The driver
let me use the phone in the back and he tried to call you on
his cell, but we couldn't get through. Jake, did you set up my
tables for me? I owe you big time, man..."

"That's okay, Tim. Where'd you get the limo?"

"Corey's Uncle Fred ordered it to take him to the airport.
I just went along for the ride." Tim set down his backpack and
whispered to Jake, "I've never done it in a limo before."

Artie said, "I'm surprised a boat that big could make the
turn onto Collingwood Street."

"It didn't. He picked us up at the Marriott. We went back
there and spent Corey's last night with the view. It was already
paid for, after all." Tim turned to Jake and added, "I'd never
done it in a suite before, either... We had a great time!"

"Artie thought you fell off a cliff or something."

Artie protested, "I wasn't worried a bit! It sounds like our
young man has had quite an adventure and I want to hear
all about it, but you have customers waiting." Tim grabbed
some menus and headed to the door to seat four women
he recognized as regulars. Then he noticed Teresa and she
introduced him to Tony, who failed to make an impression
on Tim, either.

"Now, where were we?" Artie asked. "Did you say you
two were old fans of mine?"

"Huge fans," Harley answered. "Vanessa was in show business, too. She was a dancer on Broadway and toured with some of the biggest shows. You might have seen her."

"What a thrill to meet you, Artie Glamóur. I was just a dancer in the chorus," Vanessa said. "Ever since I was a little girl it was my dream to be a Rockette, but I was too short. I still danced, though. I was in the original cast of *Oklahoma* and I was in the chorus of *Gypsy*, not with Merman, but the touring company. That was years ago, but it seems like only yesterday. I'll bet I could still *bump it with a trumpet.*"

"I'll bet you could," Artie winked and they all laughed. Then he refolded his bar towel and let out a long sigh. "Aaaaah... Finocchio's seems like only yesterday, too."

An hour later Harley and Vanessa returned to the bar after dinner to listen to Artie regale them with stories about his glory days as "Artie Glamóur," headliner at Finocchio's and the toast of North Beach, as he remembered it. Tim stared out the window and finished clearing their table. The brightest lights across Castro Street at this hour were the neon from the liquor store and the glaring white interior of the Chinese take-out. Most of the stores were closed for the night. Tim was lost in thoughts of Corey when he noticed something unusual; there was no fog tonight.

The kid might be in Chicago by now, Tim thought as he glanced at his watch. Or was it Denver? Tim had paid no attention to talk of flight schedules when that sexy young man was in his arms. Wherever it was, Corey would make his connecting flight back to Washington, D.C. and return to his normal life, whatever that was. An ambulance screamed down Castro Street toward Davies Hospital and a pair of guys in roller-derby drag skated by the window in matching cotton candy wigs. Tim figured they must be on their way to a fundraiser at Harvey's or one of the other bars.

Artie was telling about the night when Hermione Gingold came backstage after he hadn't even seen her in the audience at his show, but he stopped. The roller-derby drag kids skated by. He heard their laughter through Arts' open windows and caught a glimpse of the bright colors of their clothes and wigs, but they were long gone now. These kids skating by didn't know Artie Glamóur from Adam. They would never have heard of Hermione Gingold either. These kids today had probably forgotten who Divine was by now, too.

You could almost set your watch by the fog coming in this time of year, but not tonight. Tim watched a shirtless couple of bodybuilders walk by holding hands. They seemed in a hurry in spite of the warm night. Tim was disappointed that he couldn't even count on the fog and Artie was discouraged that the world was moving by so quickly.

Corey had been fun, but he was gone now too. He was only a boy... a big boy, but much too young for Tim. He had been sexy and comfortable and more interesting than some of the guys Tim met in the past year or so, but tonight he was just another memory to savor. Every gay man in the world seemed to pass through 18th and Castro Streets at least once in his life, so Tim was sure to see Corey again someday, maybe a year from now or maybe twenty. Tim had a job waiting tables smack dab in the middle of the Castro and lots of guys in far distant parts of the world might envy him that. He had no complaints.

"Oh, Tim!" Vanessa Caen called from the bar. Tim took another swipe across the table top with a napkin and smiled up at her. "Harley and I want to buy you a drink when you get off... or do you have other plans?"

"Sure... thanks... I should help Jake out, though, after he set up my tables for me."

"That's okay, Tim," Jake said. "It's my night to close. Hang out with your friends. I'll get even with you later."

"I'm sure you will, Jake," Tim said as he sat down at the bar.

"… and then I taught dancing for years after I retired from the stage," Vanessa was telling Artie. "Ah, there you are, Tim. What would you like to drink?"

"I'll have a vodka and tonic, please. You know, I've thought about taking a class in ballroom dancing. I've seen those contests on PBS and 'Dancing with the Stars' and they always look like they're having fun."

Jake stepped up to the bar with a tray full of dirty glasses and said to Tim, "They frown on people doing poppers at the Arthur Murray dance school, Tim."

Harley laughed, but his sister looked confused. Tim ignored Jake and asked, "What happened to Teresa? I barely met her new friend. What was his name? Tony? He seemed nice… quiet."

"They had a couple of drinks and left," Artie said.

"I think she had better plans for him than hanging around here listening to Viv torture show tunes at the piano," Jake said.

"Jake!" Artie held an index finger to his lips. "Hush! She'll hear you."

"I don't care. What's she gonna do, cross me off her Christmas card list?" Jake went to clear the last of the dinner plates. There was a crowd around the piano now and a few customers lingered over coffee and after-dinner drinks at their tables.

Vanessa and Artie carried on with tales of their show-business careers until Harley yawned enough for his sister to get the hint. "We should take you home."

"It's been a treat to get out of the house, but my energy is waning."

Artie picked up the phone and called a cab while Tim helped Harley into the wheelchair and out the door. When the taxi was about to pull away, Vanessa opened the rear window. "We'll see you at the party Friday, won't we Tim? I completely forgot to invite Artie and that was one of the reasons we came all the way over here tonight. Silly me! Please ask him to come with you, Tim."

"Friday," Tim repeated as the cab drove off. At least he knew which night it was now.

"What a delightful woman!" Artie said when Tim came back inside to finish the third drink they'd bought him.

"She was a big fan of yours, Artie," Tim said. "I didn't know you were such a celebrity."

"There's a lot the kids your age don't know. This was a whole different town back then, before AIDS and before everything got to be so expensive." Artie sighed and smiled. "Vanessa Caen... I'm so glad you brought her in here, Tim."

"I didn't bring her in, Artie. They came to meet you, not me." Tim was just glad Artie wasn't grilling him about being late for work.

"She reminded me of someone," Artie said. "No one in particular... you know what I mean? She's just the sort of person who's a stranger only once. Then every time she smiles she has the look of an old friend who shares a delicious secret."

Tim's head spun. He could hear those exact words coming from his Aunt Ruth and Artie and hadn't even met her yet. Tim suspected that he would have another night of wild dreams, but right now he just felt tired. He wasn't that much older than Corey, but Tim was worn out. "I'm glad you liked her, Artie. I almost forgot they're having a party on Friday and she asked me to invite you. Whaddayasay? You wanna come with me after I get off work?"

"I'd love to, but I can't leave Jason alone on a Friday night. What time does the party start? Maybe I can duck out early. Jason's leaving me alone on Saturday night. Maybe I should. He can cover for me for a change."

Tim had almost managed to forget about Jason. "I'm not sure. She mentioned that their friends would go on all night, although I'm sure Harley won't last long. We can talk about it tomorrow. Goodnight, Artie. Thanks again, Jake. Tell Arturo goodnight for me, will you?"

Tim intended to head straight home, but he was tired of feeling sorry for himself. Artie had been arranging things so that he and Jason never saw each other, but this had gone on long enough. When he got to the corner of 19th and Castro he turned left toward Noe Street instead of right toward Collingwood. Tim thought of all the nights he'd walked over to Jason's place on Hancock and spent the night in Jason's bed, but tonight things were different. Tim's encounter with Corey had put a sort of buffer between then and now. Tonight he would just stop by to say a friendly hello.

There was a pick-up truck in the driveway behind Jason's convertible. Tim got close enough to see a logo on the door from a nursery in Sonoma County. Jason's yard wasn't big enough for a gardener and nobody was landscaping at this hour. Tim's heart sank. Jason must have picked up some butch trick on his night off. Tim never considered that the truck might belong to someone visiting the people upstairs.

Tim felt foolish standing in the driveway. He was all ready to brag about his adventure with Corey or even admit to trying to act like Jason on Sunday, but all he really wanted tonight was a friend. Tim headed back down the hill toward the bars. As tired as he was, he wasn't ready to go home. Tim wondered where Corey was right at this moment and he tried to imagine a life more exciting than the photographs on his refrigerator. Tim stopped at the Midnight Sun, ordered a drink he didn't want and stared at the video screen. Everyone else was laughing at a scene from some old TV sitcom, but Tim's thoughts were miles away. Tim wondered if he would ever meet a great guy who wasn't too young or too old or too weird or too something...

"Hi there, Tim. Can I buy you a drink?" Tim hadn't yet taken a sip from the one in his hand and he nearly dropped it. Dave Anderson, his high school track coach, was standing right behind him.

"Yeah, it's really me. Surprised you, huh? You look good, Tim! You've filled out some since high school. You're not such a skinny kid anymore." Tim had psyched himself up to see Jason tonight; he wasn't prepared for this. Dave had been on his mind ever since that picture in the Chronicle, but Tim had convinced himself he'd only imagined it was Dave getting into that cab yesterday. His mind had been on Corey. Dave reached for his wallet. "Can I buy you a drink?" He repeated the question.

"No, I've already got one. I can't believe it's you... after all this time... I can't..." A *Saturday Night Live* spoof on the President's State of the Union address caused a roar of laughter to flood across the Midnight Sun. It was followed by an old music video of Madonna's *Express Yourself.* Tim was relieved to hear something as familiar as Madonna. It had been years since he had laid eyes on this man he once thought he knew so well. "I just can't... let's... go someplace quieter, okay?"

Neither of them spoke as they crossed Castro Street. A raucous crowd screamed approval at a drag queen's antics on the tiny stage inside Harvey's windows as they walked past. Tim tried to gauge Dave's reaction, but he couldn't. They made their way through a cluster of smokers outside the Badlands and Tim said, "I saw your picture in the paper. I thought I saw you on the corner yesterday getting into a cab. That was you, wasn't it? What are you doing here?"

"I've been looking for you. I heard you worked in a bar near 18th and Castro."

"I work in a restaurant, actually. It has a bar. But what about that preacher? Did he send you down to Castro Street to convert some fags to Jesus?"

"It's a long story."

"I've got all night," Tim said, trying to make it sound more like a threat than an invitation. He was relieved that the Edge wasn't hosting a fundraiser tonight. They crossed the room and found two stools near the back without anyone stopping Tim to talk. He had to admit that Dave looked good too. He did some quick arithmetic in his head and guessed his old coach must be in his late thirties by now. The grainy pictures in the paper didn't do him justice.

"Hi Tim… the usual?" the bartender asked.

"Make it two. I'll have whatever he's having," Dave said and reached for his wallet. "This place is nice, not too… gay. I didn't know what to expect. I guess you're a regular here."

"The Castro is like a small town, Dave, just like any small town Main Street in America, but we get more tourists than most small towns and we show them a better time." Tim shook his head, still not sure that this moment was real. In all his visions, whether in dreams or wide awake, he had never pictured seeing Dave Anderson in the flesh again. Now they were acting like a couple of old friends. "If you don't think this bar is too gay now, you should have seen it a few years back, before they remodeled. They used to have a thirty-foot shlong above the bar."

"A thirty-foot what?"

"Cock… dick… penis! They got rid of it to make room for the gay grotto up there." Tim tried to see if Dave reacted to anything, but he just kept staring at Tim, who felt like an exotic insect on the head of a pin. "What are you doing here, Dave?"

"I told you. I came looking for you."

"But why?" Tim tried to keep his voice calm. He didn't want to show any emotion.

"To apologize, I guess... to hope you could forgive me."

Tim shook his head again, as if he only imagined what he was hearing. "But what are you doing in San Francisco?"

"You said you saw the papers, so you know all about the men's rally this weekend... Arlo Montgomery?"

"I know all about Arlo Montgomery—the biggest gay-bashing bigot of them all. How did you get involved with him and how the hell do you reconcile that... with this... with looking for me?"

"I told you it's a long story, Tim. When I first met Arlo I thought he could help me. He was a therapist before he got into this religious business. It *is* a business, you know. I'd made one mistake and I thought he could help me through my problem. I had a wife and a little girl. She's a teenager now. You should see her, Tim. She's beautiful. She'll be starting college soon."

Tim cringed and took a swallow of his drink. He was glad they were at the Edge because they made the strongest drinks in town. "Yeah, she must be a little older than I was when you first met me."

Dave was oblivious to any sting in Tim's remark. "I thought Arlo could help me salvage my life. I thought I could prove I was serious about cleaning up the mess I'd made."

"Mistake! Problem! Mess!" Tim tried not to shout, but he was spitting his words out. "Is that what I was to you?"

A young man in a purple Mohawk came out of the Men's room with a roll of tape and a stack of flyers. "Fight back against the bigots! Join the protest Saturday night! The Christian Right is wrong!" he shouted as he walked toward the front door of the bar. "Defend the separation of Church and State!" He handed out flyers on the way and scattered several along the bar. One landed in front of Tim.

"What's all this?" Dave asked.

"It's a list of events to protest Arlo Montgomery and your little rally at the Civic Center this weekend. It looks like people have gotten organized in the past few days, even with the big dance party coming up on Saturday night. I'm proud of them."

"Arlo Montgomery isn't who you think he is, Tim," Dave said. "And you weren't a mistake. I was the one who made a mistake. I was wrong to deny my feelings for you and I had no business getting involved with you like that and then letting you take the blame for what happened. I'm really sorry."

"What do you want from me, Dave?" Tim asked.

"Nothing." David Anderson took a slug off his drink and spun around in his stool to put his elbows on the bar. "If you could forgive me, that would be great, but I can't ask for that. I guess I just needed to find you and see for myself that you came through it all in one piece."

"I'm fine, Dave... really. You weren't the only man who ever hurt me and I'm sure I haven't met the last." Tim turned and looked at his coach, his first lover, and he almost felt sorry for him.

"You weren't the only person I hurt either, Tim," Dave said. "I tried to go back to my wife, but there have been other guys since you. I'd learned some things, though. I never got involved with anyone as young as you were and no one who was as near to home. But there were lots of trips to Chicago, New York, Miami..."

"But how did you get mixed up with this preacher, Dave?" Tim asked.

"I told you. I thought he could help me, but he was a businessman first. He saw the power of the Christian conservatives in this country and he recognized how many strings they're able to pull in the government. He realized he could make a lot of money preying on people's fears."

"That's disgusting! It's an insult to all the decent religious people. They're not all hypocrites, you know. I've known a lot of real Christians... my Aunt Ruth, for example. Some of them even try to make the world a better place," Tim said. "San Francisco doesn't tolerate bigots. There's going to be a lot of angry people out there protesting this weekend and they're not all just gay people, either."

"I know, Tim, and I'm going to do everything I can to put a stop to it. It's the least I can do. Just think of it as my way of making it up to you, okay? None of these protests will even be necessary." Dave looked at the flyer again and shook his head.

"What do you mean?"

"I can't tell you right now, but you'll see. Trust me. Can I buy you another drink, handsome?"

Chapter 9

On Thursday morning it took Tim a minute to remember what day it was. He tried to remember how many drinks he'd put away last night and then he remembered his encounter with Dave Anderson as if it had been a dream. He forced one eye open and slid his hand across the bed, relieved to find it empty.

Tim plodded naked down the hall to put the coffee on and he opened the back door onto his patio. He felt even more relief that the fog had finally come in sometime during the night after such a rare clear evening. The gray day suited him. At least it didn't lure him to the beach. He considered going straight back to bed, but he found his newspaper at the door again and thought he should do something nice for Teresa one of these days. Sometimes he felt sorry for straight women in San Francisco, especially in the Castro. What chance did they have?

As the coffee brewed he flipped through the headlines and scanned the Bay Area section: *Some gays gear up to fight*

religious crusade while others choose to party. Tim was glad the
Chronicle ran a picture of the giant mirror ball advertising
the dance at the Moscone Center. He feared he might have
dreamed all that, too.

He flipped to Page Two of the Datebook where he
always read Jon Carroll and Leah Garchik, but Tim wasn't
awake enough to focus on them yet. Memories of last night
became clearer with his first sips of coffee. They were jumbled
together and mixed up with his horny dreams of high school
locker rooms, jock straps, track meets and his old coach Dave
Anderson.

If anyone asked, Tim would swear there was nowhere he'd
rather be than San Francisco. Even when things weren't great,
they were good. Disappointments occurred, but a terrible
day's events in Minnesota, if they happened here, would
cause one that was merely okay. Tim smiled when he thought
of Jason's old saying: "You know you've brought home the
wrong guy if you define eternity by the time between when
you cum and he goes."

There were much worse things than a lousy date, such
as a drop in his T-cells or the end of a love affair. Tim could
sometimes ease the minor pains in life with a ride on the
F-line streetcar to the Ferry Building and a long jog along the
waterfront. Some days a half an hour at the gym cleared his
head. But today Tim wished he were someplace else. Running
would only remind him of Dave Anderson. His real trouble
was that he had no one to talk to and it was his own fault.
He could have told plenty of people about his past, but he
didn't.

He knew that most San Franciscans' hearts were in the
right place. For every good cause there were people ready
to open their wallets and volunteers willing to donate their
talents and hard work, but there was one unwritten rule.
Nobody would tolerate a bore. For every sad coming-out

story, there was a sadder one, a more homophobic father in an even smaller, more conservative town. Tim's experience with Dave ranked at next to nothing compared to some of the horror stories he'd heard. He carried his coffee to the living room, sat down by the bay window and flicked on the computer. There was only one person who knew what Tim had been through and she would always listen.

Dear Aunt Ruth—

Sorry I didn't answer your e-mail right away. I had a champion hangover that day, but this morning's is running a close second. Don't worry. I'm not ready for the Betty Ford clinic yet. I don't want you to worry about me at all, but I know you will, so I might as well come out with it.

I saw Dave Anderson last night! He tracked me down in my own neighborhood. I guess he was trying to be nice in his own way, but the weirdest thing was—he almost seemed to be coming on to me too, after all this time. He looked good, but I'm proud to say I resisted his advances. I'm probably flattering myself. I'm too old for him now, anyway.

Arlo Montgomery arrives here tomorrow and the gays are up in arms, but Dave says he is going to put a stop to everything. I think he's delusional, but he wouldn't explain, so I don't know what he has in mind. How could he have the power? And he said it like he was doing it for me, as if that would make everything all right between us, like some kind of atonement. He's nuts, if you ask me. One thing I know for sure, he's never going back to Nancy.

Aunt Ruth, I know you're concerned about me and I love you for it. I do meet lots of guys my own age every day, but there's rarely any spark. I fell kinda hard for this bartender named Jason where I work, but that didn't pan out. I hope we can be friends someday, but I haven't even seen him lately.

Then last weekend I met a college kid from Washington D.C. who was a lot of fun, but he was only here for a visit. My friend Jake at work says relationships are like your favorite shoes or your favorite blue jeans. When you get them broken in enough to feel comfortable they start falling apart. Jake shouldn't complain. He does all right, but it's been a long time since I've gotten past that 'newly stiff' stage with blue jeans, if you know what I mean, and you can take that however you like.

I can't wait for you to come and visit. The guys at work will love you—Artie and Arturo are an older gay couple that own the restaurant and they're also my landlords. Jake and Patrick are a little crazy, but they're nice enough and Viv, the piano player… well, you'll see. I have some vacation time coming too, so I can show you around. We'll have fun and of course there's room for you to stay with me. You can even have my bed and I'll sleep on the couch. I take naps on it sometimes and it's real comfortable. If I come home with a trick, though, you might have to sleep there. I've got an idea! We'll make it a contest. Whoever brings a man home first takes the bed and the other one gets the couch. See you soon!

Love, Tim

Tim clicked SEND and took another sip of coffee. It was cold, so he chugged it and headed for the shower. Maybe it was the smell of soap or the needle on the bathroom scale that showed an extra pound, but Tim decided to go for a run after all. It would be a good break from his tedious gym routine. He poked his head out the back door as he towel-dried his hair. The fog was burning off and his hangover had abated too. He pulled on a jock strap and baggy running shorts with a sexy slit up both sides. Then he scrounged under the bed for his favorite running shoes. He thought of Jake's comment again. These shoes were about as comfortable as shoes could be and Tim hoped they didn't fall apart for a long time.

Tim found his jacket from last night and shook it upside down to empty the pockets. His keys fell out as well as a square tan envelope that landed between his pillows. It was the size of a *Thank You* note and Tim knew he hadn't put it there. He wondered if Dave Anderson had written him a formal apology, but that seemed out of character. Whatever it was, Dave must have slipped it into Tim's pocket when he went to the toilet at the Edge. He tore it open, not sure whether to be excited or angry. Whatever Dave had to say, he could have said to his face. Inside, he found a receipt and a note: *Tim—If anything happens to me, take this to the airport and it will prove everything. Don't use it unless you absolutely have to—Dave.*

Tim wasn't sure whether or not his old coach was crazy, but there was one thing that seemed certain; Dave Anderson sounded a little scared.

Tim ran north to Oak Street and jogged through the panhandle of Golden Gate Park. He felt out of shape before he reached Stanyan Street. He was used to a few laps around Dolores Park, but this was the longest he'd run since placing among the first ten thousand in the annual Bay-to-Breakers race in May. He remembered how he ached that week, but how proud he was at having finished. A bunch of guys he knew from the gym had run Bay-to-Breakers naked and almost talked Tim into joining them. As he ran passed Marlena's, the only gay bar on the route, a crowd of people hooted and called his name. It was Artie and Arturo and a whole gang of regulars from Arts. Thank God he wasn't naked!

Today was a perfect San Francisco day—warm in the sun with a cool breeze. Men in hardhats, boots and coveralls lined JFK Drive. Tim stared at one so hard he ran into the path of a sprinkler and then stepped into a puddle that splashed mud up his leg. The sexy workman turned away just in time to miss Tim's clumsiness. Then he remembered that these guys were doing their jobs and not out here for a Village People look-alike contest. Construction never seemed to end. First they tore down and rebuilt the DeYoung Museum. Then it was the Academy of Sciences. Tim hoped no one planned to bulldoze the Japanese Tea Garden to make it more modern. For the biggest piece of pristine open space in the city, Golden Gate Park was always under construction, but so was the rest of the city. Construction workers were almost as plentiful as tourists.

There might be towns in America that stayed the same year after year. Tim remembered them from his Minnesota childhood as passing scenes from the back seat with the car windows open, smelling of bakeries and new mown lawns. They were jigsaw puzzles with all their pieces in place or completed paint-by-numbers of Americana. Their colors might fade over time, but otherwise they remained the same. If San Francisco was a work of art it was one that would never be finished.

Tim thought about his earlier conversation with Arturo. Yes, he and Jason might be finished and Tim was growing to accept that, but his own life was just getting into gear. He felt a surge of energy and picked up his pace past the rose gardens. Kids were on a field trip led by teachers who couldn't be much more than Tim's age. They petted a live iguana on the grass, a creature that only existed in books when Tim was in school.

He ran clockwise around the outer rim of Stow Lake and crossed the arched bridge onto the island and Strawberry Hill. Tim sat on a bench beside the waterfall and read the plaque: *Doreen Querido, Artist – Activist – Lesbian, 1947 – 1997*. A turtle the size of Tim's foot climbed onto the bank and stared up at him. Tim tried to remember his high school Spanish. *Querido* must a form of the verb *querer*, to want or desire and he felt some kinship with another gay person, even though she was a woman he never knew.

He wished he had something to feed the turtle, but he would probably only scare it away. Doreen Querido had only lived to be fifty. Some benches in Golden Gate Park were dedicated to people whose entire lives happened before Tim was born. He'd seen plaques that bore the names of two men who died in the 1980s—lovers, partners, AIDS victims? He wondered how long he would get to live here. His current HIV drugs seemed to be working fine. Maybe he would get to have a long life just like normal people. Tim took a hit off a joint and thought he saw the turtle yawn at him before it plopped back under the water and swam away.

A pair of young men walked past him pushing a baby carriage. Tim was jealous until he heard the baby cry. He envied their commitment more than their responsibilities. He saw two cute guys in a paddleboat in the distance and Tim forgot about parenting and the names on brass plaques on park benches. It had been two whole days since he'd had sex with… what was his name? Oh yeah… Corey.

"Hey Tim!" One of the guys in the paddleboat was waving at him.

"Hi Patrick! I didn't recognize you outside of work." It was the newest waiter at Arts, the one they all wanted not to like. He was too perfect, blonde and blue-eyed with a great body and straight white teeth. Jake had said Patrick reminded him of a Ken doll or a figure on top of a wedding cake. And Patrick seemed to evaluate every move in terms of its political correctness. Tim agreed with Patrick's politics, but his earnestness grew tiresome. Still, it was hard to dislike someone so eager and guileless.

"This is my friend Barry. Barry, this is Tim. We work together at Arts."

"Hi, Barry. Nice day for a boat ride." Tim waved. They were too far from shore to shake hands. Barry was sexy... or was Tim just horny? He was never sure lately.

"You working tonight, Tim?"

"Yeah, you?"

"I'm coming in after the dinner rush. Artie wants to train me to fill in behind the bar when they're short. Tonight he's going to teach me to close so I can do it by myself."

"Why's that?" Tim asked. "Where is everybody going?"

"Jason is working that big party at the Moscone Center on Saturday. I'm taking off that night for the demonstration at the Civic Center."

Tim didn't want to suggest that if David Anderson was telling the truth about foiling Arlo Montgomery's plans, the demonstration might not be necessary.

"And Artie said he's going to a party with you tomorrow night."

"Oh, yeah. I almost forgot. See you tonight," Tim said. It was time to head back, anyway. Tim was hungry and thirsty and needed to get ready for work. At least his hangover was gone.

"Where have you been all day?" Artie asked Tim as soon as he walked in the door of the restaurant. "Some guy was looking for you, ringing your doorbell at the apartment and then he came by here not half an hour ago."

"I went jogging in Golden Gate Park," Tim said, feeling defensive. He couldn't imagine that Dave Anderson would have come back to see him so soon after leaving him that note last night. "Who was he?"

"His name sounded like a girl... something like Genevieve..."

Jake piped up, "That flight attendant, Tim... the French one... you know."

"Oh! Great! Jean-Yves?" Tim asked. "I haven't seen him since last fall."

"Jean-Yves—Genevieve... I was close," Artie said.

"What did he want?" Tim asked.

"He wanted you! What do you mean by that? 'Oh, great?' He was adorable—a little younger than you're used to, but not as young as that kid you had last weekend. What was his name? Cary? This one had the cutest French accent. I've always been a sucker for accents. I remember when Arturo used to come back from visiting his relatives in Nicaragua and roll his 'R's. It drove me wild, but it never lasted."

"Tim doesn't mind a little foreign tongue once in a while, do you?" Jake was standing behind him at the waiters' station and pretended to stick his tongue in Tim's ear.

"Corey," Tim corrected Artie and sidestepped his co-worker.

"I thought you said Jean-Yves." Artie was confused.

"Jean-Yves is the name of the French flight attendant," Tim said to Jake. "And Artie, the boy I *had* last weekend was Corey, not Cary. Don't we have anything to do around here besides talk about my sex life?"

Tim did feel "great" about the news that Jean-Yves was in town again, but he didn't want it to be everyone else's business. He and Jean-Yves had met a while back and though they didn't keep in touch, the sexy Frenchman would show up when he had a layover in San Francisco. Tim thought one of the best things about being gay in the 21st century was the ability to have men like Jean-Yves in his life. He might have a lover in every port, but Tim didn't care. Jean-Yves had insisted on safe sex from the beginning and in some ways they had more fun than the guys Tim got bent out of shape over, like Jason. Tim knew from the very first time that they were never going to be *domestic partners*, so he was open to just having fun with Jean-Yves whenever he came to town. This news put Tim in a good mood all evening. Even the most demanding customers didn't bother him and the dinner shift flew past. As Tim bent over the table to pick up his last tip of the night he felt a hand on his ass and heard a familiar voice whisper something sexy in French.

Chapter 10

When Tim woke up on Friday morning a muscular arm was draped around him. Jean-Yves never fell asleep without his watch, but it was set to Paris time, so Tim craned his neck to get a look at the alarm clock on his bedside table. It wasn't quite seven. He'd left the window open enough to hear birds arguing on the roof. Jean-Yves' regular breathing meant he was still fast asleep.

Jean-Yves also never reset his stomach as he traveled through time zones. He sometimes ordered a cheeseburger for breakfast or eggs for dinner. What did Tim care? Last night was just what he needed. The last time Jean-Yves was in San Francisco was before Tim started sleeping with Jason and this time was just after Corey. Tim didn't care to count how many men there had been in between. In the months since they'd seen each other, Jean-Yves seemed bigger than Tim remembered. He must find time to work out, even on his strange schedule.

Tim extricated himself from Jean-Yves, went to the bathroom and then looked through the peephole in his front door for the morning paper. He must be up before Teresa for a change. He turned on the coffee maker, pulled on a robe and stepped into the hallway in his bare feet.

Due to the slope of the hill, Tim's apartment was the only one on the ground floor. The room across the hall was just large enough for five water heaters, three washing machines, two dryers and a clothesline. The tenants felt lucky when all the washers worked, but Arturo and Artie never raised the rent, so no one complained much. Tim grabbed both Chronicles and bounded up the stairs. Classical music came from the apartment of the newest tenant, Malcolm. Tim didn't think he would even recognize him if they met on the street.

Ben and Jane Larson lived across the hall from Malcolm. They were the "token straights" in the building and they had a little girl named Sarah. Tim heard a television tuned to a children's show and Sarah was happily singing along. At the top of the stairs he was about to drop Teresa's paper at her door when it opened. "Tim! You startled me. I was just going to run downstairs for that."

"I thought I'd beat you to it for a change. Here."

"I'd invite you in for coffee, but Tony's just getting ready to leave."

Tim thought she looked sleepy in her tattered robe and bare feet. "That's okay, Teresa. I've got my own coffee going and someone waiting for me too."

"Now, why doesn't that surprise me?" Teresa asked with a sly smirk.

Tim could hear snippets of a man's voice coming from Teresa's television set and it wasn't tuned to *Sesame Street.* "*The Day of Judgment is coming…. forty-five million babies murdered, all in the name of a woman's right to choose… heathen liberals care more about a beached whale or the habitat of an insect... more about the rights of the sodomites... than the lives of the innocent unborn!"*

"What the hell are you watching, Teresa?"

"It's the local news. They're showing that nutty preacher that's coming to town."

"Where will you stand, my friends? Will you stand on the right hand of the Lord or... "

"I'm not watching it...I just turned on the television set in the kitchen when I went in to make coffee."

"...cast into the fiery pits of eternal damnation? Our great nation was..."

"I've got to go turn this off right now!" Teresa said. "Thanks for the paper."

"You bet... Seeya later."

Tim ran downstairs and turned on the TV set in his own kitchen to get a good look at Arlo Montgomery, but the newscast went to a live shot on Castro Street. The reporter was getting reactions from commuters above Harvey Milk plaza. The camera angle had the Castro Theatre in the background. Tim recognized a guy he'd gone home with a couple of months ago, but he slipped past and the reporter picked someone else for a comment, someone who looked dazed and could barely formulate an intelligent sentence. Either the eloquent gay commuters weren't out this morning or they didn't want their faces on television.

Tim picked up the small square envelope from beside the toaster. He opened it, fingered the receipt and read Dave Anderson's note again. The local news went back to the studio. *"Several protesters will greet the arrival of Arlo Montgomery at the airport this afternoon. The minister urges his followers to support politicians in repealing gay rights legislation across the country. Meanwhile, thousand of gays arrive in San Francisco this weekend for what is being billed as the party of the decade at the Moscone Center…"*

Tim glanced at the clock on the microwave. He dropped Dave's note back into the envelope as he watched the mirror ball dangling from the helicopter on the morning news. He wanted to get dressed and head to the airport right now. He could find out what the receipt was for and then join the protesters. Tim heard a yawn and a naked man stepped into the kitchen. "What are you watching? What time is it?" Jean-Yves' accent was thicker than usual when he was half-asleep.

"Haven't you heard? This jerk is arriving in San Francisco today. We could go to the airport right now for the protest."

"Oh, yes… I've heard all about him," Jean-Yves said. "You go ahead. I spend enough time in airports. Americans are crazy!"

Tim's anger was rising at the same rate as his libido. "What do you mean by crazy? Don't you think we should protest when people try to take away our rights? Don't you think we need to fight back?"

"Take it easy," Jean-Yves said as he put his arms around Tim's shoulders. "I'm on your side. I didn't mean you were crazy, amoureux. I don't think of San Francisco like the rest of America, do you?"

"No, but…" Tim calmed down.

"I just meant that Americans are up-tight about sex," Jean-Yves explained. "The people who aren't getting any are always jealous of the ones who are, so they want to put a stop to it and make the sexy people's lives as miserable as their own."

"I guess that makes sense, especially when I hear it with a French accent." Tim smiled.

"Trust me! Any straight guys coming to San Francisco this weekend to listen to bad music and hear this Montgomery preach hellfire and brim soles, rather than spending the time with his wife or his girlfriend, isn't getting any."

"I think you mean 'brimstone,' but I'm sure you're right."

"Oh course I am right, mon amoureux beau... Besides, there's a big dance tomorrow night at the Moscone place. That's why I scheduled this time in San Francisco, to go to the party... and to see you, of course. You are coming, aren't you? I have friends coming from all over the world, but I will save for you the last dance of the night if you like me to."

"I have to work tomorrow night," Tim said. "Maybe I'll come later, if I don't go to the Civic Center and get arrested instead. I've got to go to the gym too, before I go to any party and take my shirt off."

Jean-Yves stroked Tim's chest. "Your pecs are fine."

Tim nuzzled his face against the muscular ripples of Jean-Yves' stomach without standing up from the kitchen chair.

"Come on, my beautiful San Francisco friend. Come back to your bed. You don't want to be one of those poor frustrated Americans that's not getting any—not while I'm around."

The first moments alone after a night of good sex were always prickly. Tim wasn't used to spending the whole night with another body in his bed, but he liked it. Now that Jean-Yves had left after another "rencontre sexuels" this morning and a quick shower, Tim's apartment was much too quiet, especially the bedroom. Even the noisy birds outside above the air well had taken their squabbles elsewhere.

Jean-Yves went to meet friends for lunch downtown so Tim went to the gym to work out, had a protein shake for lunch and still had plenty of time for a nap before work. He thought he might not be horny again for hours.

Chapter 11

Artie was whistling and cutting limes when Tim arrived at the restaurant. Tim was feeling pretty good too, but his mood was a far cry from whistling. "What's up, Artie?" Tim asked as he glanced at the reservation book.

"*We're* going to a big party tonight! Don't tell me you forgot!"

"Oh, yeah... that."

"Tim! I've been looking forward to this party for the past two days. Don't give me that 'oh, yeah...' attitude. You *did* forget, didn't you?"

"I didn't forget the party, Artie," Tim protested. "I just wasn't thinking about it this very minute."

"Do you mean you were planning to go to the party dressed like that...in your waiter drag?"

"Artie, I can change after work. We both just live around the corner..."

"I know, but I thought since Patrick is coming in to close for me... Jake can finish up your tables if there are any stragglers. The minute it slows down here I want you to run home and put on something festive and sexy. I have a change of clothes in the office. I know the only reason they invited me is because they want to see Artie Glamóur, but I can't fit into any of my old drag. I suppose I could have worn a caftan, but that's so 60s!"

"I'm sure they'll like you just fine, Artie." Tim *had* nearly forgotten about Harley Wagner and Vanessa. He supposed the party might not be so bad, but Tim wondered what Jean-Yves was doing tonight. It always seemed like the more he got the more he wanted. Tim didn't imagine there'd be anyone he knew at the party besides Artie and the hosts, but in San Francisco you never could tell what characters might cross your path.

The restaurant was busy, even for a Friday night. There were droves of tourists in town for the Moscone Center party on Saturday. Artie and Patrick were both busy behind the bar. Artie working at top speed was only about half of Jason's normal rate, so Tim and Jake were glad Patrick was there to take up the slack. Tim ordered four Margaritas and found a moment to ask him how it went at the airport.

"It was fun. About a hundred of us went out on BART and a couple dozen more drove their cars and brought banners and signs... salt or no salt?"

"Salt on three... one without... So did you get to see Arlo Montgomery? Did you get up in his face? How about the press? Were you on the evening news?" Tim looked up to see one of the television sets above the bar showing 'Jeopardy' with closed captioning, but nobody was watching. Viv hated the television stealing attention away from her piano, anyway.

"There were a couple of camera crews, but Montgomery flew into SFO on a private jet, so we couldn't get near him."

"That's too bad..." Jake piped up. He was waiting for drinks now, too.

"Yeah, you'd think someone would have checked that out beforehand, but it was still a great day." Patrick seemed cheerful in spite of their plans being thwarted. "The cops were everywhere and there should be pictures in the papers, at least the B.A.R. and the Chronicle. Some of the local TV channels had cameras there, but they went live with that big fire in San Jose for most of the 6:00 news... maybe at 10 or 11."

"You'll have to let me know," Tim said.

"It doesn't matter. At least we know people are willing to turn out. They'll all be at the Civic Center tomorrow night and there's no way Arlo Montgomery can avoid a confrontation there. A bunch of us guys are going to dress up like straight people and infiltrate the place."

"What about tonight?" Tim asked. "Why wait until tomorrow?"

"Tonight is only the warm-up," Patrick explained. "Arlo Montgomery won't even be there. He's probably holed up in a suite at the Fairmont sipping champagne with a high-class hooker. Tonight they're giving them gospel choirs and second-string wannabe preachers."

"I see," Tim said as he whisked the tray of Margaritas to his table. He wondered where Dave Anderson fit into the opening night picture and if Dave really had something up his sleeve to stop this whole thing from happening.

There was a line at the door waiting for tables now and most of the customers seemed to be tourists. Viv was ecstatic at the crowd around her piano. In order to stave off needing a potty break while the tips were flowing, she didn't ask Tim to get her a drink all evening. By the time things slowed

down, she was on her third rendition of *San Francisco* and Tim
noticed that it was 10:30.

He ran home and took a quick shower, then pulled on a
bright red, short-sleeved shirt with a tight pair of blue jeans.
The shirt clung in all the right places and showed off his arms,
but it wasn't too dressy. He grabbed his black leather jacket. If
the party was boring he could skip out early and hit some bars,
since he'd be South of Market anyway. Artie was standing
beside a cab in front of the restaurant when Tim came back
around the corner. "Hurry up! The meter is running. What
took you so long?"

Tim was relieved to see Artie dressed all in black. "Sorry,
Artie. I didn't know you were getting a cab. I thought we were
taking the streetcar."

"Don't be silly, Tim! I wanted to take our car, but Arturo
wouldn't hear of me driving after I had a few cocktails.

It wasn't until they climbed inside the cab that Tim noticed
the full effect of Artie's transformation by the unflattering
light of the dome lamp. He had on just a hint of mascara and
a rope of pearls that wrapped twice around his neck and fell
halfway down his chest across what looked like a black satin
Nehru jacket. "You look nice, Tim," Artie said right away.

Tim was stunned for a moment, but knew that a return of
the compliment was expected. "Thanks… you too, Artie."

"I *do not*. I'd too damned fat! Clementina and 8th Street,
please," Artie yelled across the seat toward the driver.

"Are those real pearls?" Tim asked.

"Of course not!" Artie said. "They're not worth much
more than Mardi gras beads. What kind of fool do you think I
am? I wouldn't risk wearing real pearls South of Market. The
last time I was down there that neighborhood was still pretty
dicey."

"Harley's apartment is nice, though," Tim said. "It's huge! Of course, I've never been there at night, so it will probably seem very different."

Artie wasn't listening. He was wiggling his fingers on both hands until Tim noticed the rings. "The diamonds are real," Artie said before he turned them around toward his palms again so that only the silver bands were showing. "They're insured, but I'll wait until we're safe inside before I show them off."

Tim felt claustrophobic with someone of Artie's girth inside the cramped elevator as it creaked and groaned to the top. He could have taken the stairs faster. A butler pulled back the iron grill and Vanessa met them right inside. She was dressed in silver and black with a champagne flute in one hand. "Artie Glamóur!" she squealed. "What a thrill to see you! She kissed him on both cheeks and turned to Tim. "And Timothy Snow. My, how handsome you look! Come right this way. The last time I saw Harley he was on the deck, trying to offer a joint to Willie Brown. He'll be so glad to see you both, but stop at the bar and get yourselves a drink first."

They waited for a pair of men to pass in the narrow hallway. Both had hairless white asses protruding like ripe melons from their black leather chaps. "Hi, Tim!" they said in unison. Where had he seen them before? Artie glared at Tim, but he couldn't remember. The mirrored wall Vanessa had talked about on Tim's first visit was open now to reveal the bar. A bare-chested man in black slacks and a bow-tie poured drinks. Tim was wondering where Harley had found this sexy bartender when a woman shouted from across the living room. "Artie Glamóur! Is that really you?"

"Carol!" Artie yelled back. "Tim… fetch me a scotch on the rocks as soon as this gorgeous stud gets caught up behind the bar. I haven't seen Carol since we both worked in North

Beach! Bring my drink over and I'll introduce you two...
Carol Doda, as I live and breathe!"

Tim watched Artie air-kiss his old friend. He wondered
who she was and almost forgot why he was standing there
until the handsome bartender asked, "What can I get you,
cutie?" This party might be all right after all.

"I'd like a scotch... on the rocks... please," Tim said, "Oh...
and a vodka and tonic for me." The bartender reminded Tim
of Jason, but a little bit shorter and stockier. He probably knew
Jason. Didn't everyone? San Francisco seemed like such a
small town sometimes. Hell, this guy and Jason had probably
already done it together—twice. Still, he didn't seem to know
Tim. At least he didn't ask Tim where Jason was. Tim was
growing used to that question by now.

Instead, the bartender asked, "You just getting here,
babe?"

"Yeah, I had to work. The guy with the pearls is my boss.
They're not real, but the diamonds are..." Why was he talking
so much? He was nervous, that was why. He could sure use
a joint and that shouldn't be too difficult to find at this party.
Tim forced his eyes away from the bartender's hairy chest
to look at his watch. "Jeez, it's almost midnight. Is the party
winding down?"

Mr. Hairy Muscular Pecs managed to brush his fingertips
across Tim's knuckles while he set down the drinks. "No, it's
just getting started. There must have been fifty people arrive
in the last twenty minutes. Harley has hired me to work his
parties before... believe me, after the bars close at 2am this
place will get packed. I'm scheduled to work until at least
five."

"Too bad... that you have to work so late," Tim said.

"I'm Matthew. What's your name?"

"Tim... Tim Snow."

"Hey, Tim. I'll see you later, but here's my card, just in case I don't get a chance to talk with you again... call me sometime." He winked.

By the time Tim delivered his scotch, Artie was surrounded by well-wishers. They all seemed to know him and one another. Tim had seen a couple of drag queens in line at the bar, but the fans who flocked around Artie were a more mature and mixed crowd. "There you are, Tim." Artie reached across a feather boa-ed shoulder for his drink. "I was afraid you got lost in the arms of that stud behind the bar. Carol... this is my escort, Tim. Tim Snow, I'd like you to meet the fabulous Miss Carol Doda. We used to be neighbors."

"How do you do," Tim shook the retired stripper's delicate hand, though it was hard to take his eyes away from her breasts. "Did you used to live on Collingwood too?"

She just laughed and Artie explained, "No, silly boy... We were neighbors at our jobs! Carol was the headliner at the Condor Club at Broadway and Columbus when I was at Finocchio's up the street. And these are my old friends Benny and Cornell." Introductions went on and Tim just kept smiling. He could deal with the public at work, but he felt shy at parties and was terrible with names until he got to know people. Artie seemed to know them all.

Music poured in from the patio as well as a steady stream of people coming and going. The deck seemed larger than it had at lunch the other day. Tables were covered with tiers of hors d'oeuvres and beyond the tallest plants was an open-air dance floor with a ceiling of laser beams above the dancers. "Tim! Over here!" It was Harley with a joint at his lips, thank goodness. He sat perched on a stool where he could survey his guests. Harley gave Tim a hug and passed the joint.

Tim knew well enough by now to take only one small toke before he handed it back to Harley, who acted as if the stuff

didn't even faze him. Harley smiled at the cautious grin on
Tim's face. The bass beat moved up through the soles of Tim's
shoes and a high sweet voice filled his head. "This sounds like
Aretha Franklin. Or is it Patti LaBelle?" Tim asked.

"Neither," said Harley. "I asked the DJ to play some
Sylvester to get folks warmed up for the party tomorrow
night."

"That's right," Tim said. "I knew that... Wow, I'm stoned
already. I almost forgot about the party tomorrow what with
work and all. Today's only Friday, right?"

"Actually, Tim, it's past midnight now, so it's Saturday.
Come with me. I want to show you something." Harley
reached for a cane behind him. The wheelchair was out of
sight and Tim was startled to see how tall Harley was when
he stood. Tim turned back to watch Artie twirl Vanessa in the
midst of a group of drag queens and men in leather. Artie's
beads swung around his head as his lips moved to the words:
"Get on your feet and dance to the beat and dance!" Tim had never
seen Artie look happier.

"This way, Tim." Harley led him back across the crowded
living room. They excused themselves as they passed more
guests and cut through the kitchen where Matthew gave
Tim another wink. A pair of bare-chested waiters loaded
silver trays of hot hors d'oeuvres from the oven. More guests
arrived, some coming up the stairs, now. Tim was amazed to
see five laughing people tumble out of the elevator all at once.
How did they manage to fit in there?

"Did you ever feel that you had a purpose in life, Tim?"
Harley asked. He had led Tim down a long hallway and
they entered a bedroom now. One section of the wall near
the window was covered in framed photographs of a much
younger-looking Harley with the same man in each of them.
"Did you ever ask yourself why you were put here on this
planet?" There was the Eiffel Tower. There they were in front

of the Taj Majal and the Sphinx. They ice-skated arm-in-arm on the famous rink at Rockefeller Center. In another shot they were on skis with Lake Tahoe a deep pool of blue in the distant background. Tim thought of the snapshots he'd been showing to Corey on his refrigerator at home, but these framed photographs seemed to put his life's meager adventures to shame.

"I'm sorry Harley. What did you say?" These questions were more than Tim wanted to contemplate right now. What was going on here? Was Harley going to try to seduce him? Tim thought Harley was nice and he liked him and everything, but not that way.

"I just wondered if you ever thought about why we're here," Harley said softly. "You know… fate and destiny and all that?"

"Not really, Harley. Gee, I'm not even thirty, yet. I always thought there would be plenty of time to figure out all that stuff… all in good time, right? I'm just trying to enjoy life, not analyze it too much. Where was this picture taken? Who is this guy you were with? You're both so hot!"

"Tokyo," he answered. "That was my lover, Bill. We thought we were the luckiest guys in the world and maybe we were. When I met Bill it was like someone finally saw the real me for the first time in my life. We discovered each other like long-lost friends. We were even younger than you are now and he was so handsome, but most of all he looked at me and he *knew* me. Has anyone ever really *known* you, Tim? Have you ever let anyone know the real you?"

"I'm not sure I know what you mean, Harley…"

Harley took a deep breath and picked up a photograph from the bedside table. "Bill loved to travel and I went along for the ride. I would have gone anywhere to be with him. I never wondered why. I didn't ask questions. Neither did he. We thought there'd be plenty of time for that—for whatever came our way—lots of time. We were young. He didn't even live long enough to get sick or to see me get sick or to witness the horrible decline of any of our friends. He died so quickly, so very quickly. He was gone like the light when you flick off a switch."

"I'm sorry, Harley… what happened?"

"It was a car accident, three blocks from here. Can you believe it? Drunk driver, broad daylight. I was home making dinner and I heard the sirens, but I had no idea…"

"I'm so sorry, Harley."

"Yeah, me too. I was sorry, but I was mostly jealous. I'd think of his death and crave it like a drug. I thought about how much easier it would be to die in an instant than to suffer missing him. I resented him for not having to endure what the rest of us did, especially when AIDS hit. Bill and I always thought whatever happened we'd get through it together. Sometimes things just don't turn out the way you plan." Harley lit another joint and passed it to Tim. "Bill would have a fit if he saw me smoking inside the house. Fuck it! He can't tell me what to do."

"I've probably had enough, Harley. This stuff is strong," Tim said before he took a deep hit.

"This last time I was in the hospital was the worst, Tim. That's when I got to thinking I'd never really done anything to leave a lasting impression on the world. I wasn't sure if I would come home from the hospital that time, but if I did there was one thing I *could* do that might change things for the better." Harley reached into the drawer of the bedside table and brought out a gun.

Tim's vision was flooded with his dream about Alcatraz. Vanessa Caen was in the roller coaster ahead of him beside a tall man with a gun. Now Harley Wagner held that gun in his right hand. Tim was stoned, but he knew this wasn't a dream and he was scared of what would happen next.

"There you are, Harley!" Vanessa opened the door and joined them. "Are you tired, dear? So many new guests have arrived and they're all asking about you. We wondered where you'd disappeared to."

Sounds from the party rushed in before she could close the door again—the bass beat, a scream of laughter, a cocktail glass breaking on a tile floor, but Tim was still transfixed by the sight of the gun. Someone moaned nearby, maybe in a bedroom next-door, a man's voice growling, "Yeah, you want it, don't you? Hungry boy! Take it all... Yeah, boy! Take it..."

"Hello Vanessa. Come on in. I was just about to tell Tim about our plans."

"Oh my, I suppose it's time we had a little talk with Tim, isn't it..." Vanessa came around the bed and sat on Harley's left, accepting the joint. He held the gun in his right hand beside his face exactly as it was on the roller coaster. Tim gasped and Vanessa said, "Come and sit down beside me here, Tim. Are you all right?"

"This is just like in my dream," Tim tried to explain, but his body felt frozen, too heavy to move any closer. "I had a dream and there was a party in it, but the party was on Alcatraz. My dream was the same night after that first day I was here, so I hadn't even met Harley yet, but we were all on a Ferris Wheel and then it turned into a roller coaster and I could only see the back of your heads and Harley, you were holding the gun just like you are now and there was this boy and girl behind me that I met on the subway on my way home that day and he had a switchblade knife in my dream and..."

"Are you taking any medications, Tim?" Harley interrupted. "It's none of my business, but you know some of the AIDS drugs cause intense dreams. And it sounds like you might be a little bit clairvoyant."

"Yeah, I guess so," Tim said. "I mean... yes. I take the drugs and they used to say my grandmother was a psychic. I barely remember her, but I have a picture of us when I was a little boy at Powderhorn Park on the fourth of July. I wanted to know more about her, but whenever she came up they changed the subject, like it was something to be ashamed of. I have dreams all the time…"

"There's nothing wrong with dreams, dear, but Harley and I need to tell you a little story and make a confession, now." Vanessa moved around to Tim's side of the bed and took his hand. "Please sit down… That day I met you on the streetcar was not entirely an accident, you know. Your leading us back to Artie was merely a lucky coincidence, but that day we met I was looking for just the right sort of person to help Harley with his plan… "

"Do you mean when you stumbled, when you landed in my lap that wasn't an accident?"

"I was trained as a dancer, dear, but I've done a bit of acting too."

"Your ankle…"

"No, I didn't twist it at all, dear Timothy. My ankle was just fine, but I wanted to see if you would offer to help me."

"Do I really need to know all this right now? Couldn't it wait? That grass is so strong." Tim felt a little better when Harley placed the gun back inside the drawer and closed it, but he didn't think he could process any more information right now. He could barely speak.

"I'm sorry, Tim," Harley said. "You see, tonight was supposed to be my bon voyage party, but things have changed, now."

"Maybe we should back up to that day on the streetcar, Harley," Vanessa sat down between the two of them. "Timothy, you need to understand that Harley had just returned home from the hospital and we didn't know how long he'd be with us. The tests weren't conclusive, but they hadn't been good in a long time. We thought he might only have a few more weeks and I was looking for just the right person to help Harley with his plan."

"What plan?"

"Well, as I was saying before Vanessa came into the room, I never figured out any good reason for my life, for my being here."

"That's just silly, Harley," his sister said. "You've been a wonderful friend to so many people and you've been just as solid as a rock for me—so strong at those times in my life when I needed you. And don't forget that Bill loved you very much."

"All that is beside the point, Nessa... What I'm trying to explain to Tim is that since I was about to die anyway and I hadn't done anything important in life... to *my* way of thinking, at least... I wanted my death to be of value to someone. That was when I heard about Arlo Montgomery coming to town. I was watching the television news in my hospital bed and I was hooked up to so many tubes I felt helpless and I vowed right then and there that if I ever got out of that hospital again..."

"I was right there beside him when he thought of this, I was..." Vanessa said.

"Don't interrupt me, sis," Harley scolded, lifting the fingertip that had been on the trigger a moment ago. "I lied to you, Tim, when I said I would have chosen to go to the party at the Moscone Center. Sure, a part of me would, but this was one thing I could do to make a difference. Arlo Montgomery was not only preaching hatred in the name of God, but he was preying on the worst of people's fears. He rakes in their money and uses it to buy power, or at least the attention of those who have power. So much of our progress could be set back by these phony Christians like Arlo Montgomery. I thought of all of my friends who have died and all of the enemies who still live. If Bill or any one of our friends had known exactly when their time would come they each could have taken out one of those bastards with them. I knew that I was dying soon and I decided I could make the world a better place by taking Arlo Montgomery with me."

"Wow, Harley. I can hardly believe this... but what about me?" Tim asked. "Why did you need my help? Why couldn't you just get your sister to help you?"

"They don't allow women into those revival meetings," Vanessa said. "They're like stag parties—MEN ONLY! Can you believe such a thing in this day and age?"

"But what about me?" Tim asked again. "Why did you want to involve me in all this?"

Harley relit the joint and passed it to his sister before he went on, "I needed to find someone innocent—someone without a motive—and someone strong. That was the whole idea. I needed someone who knew nothing about my plan so there was no way they could implicate you."

"But how were you going to get close enough to Arlo Montgomery to shoot him?" Tim still didn't believe what he was hearing.

"Who would question a helpless old man? The wheelchair is too wide to fit through the metal detectors and there's enough metal in it that one of those wand scanners wouldn't detect the gun if I had it tucked under a blanket in my lap. The handicapped section is right down in front. You were going to push me inside and then I'd send you out on an errand. I might have forgotten my pills or asked you to make a phone call—any reason to get you out of the way. After I shot him there would have been pandemonium. They wouldn't let you back in and if I took a bullet right then and there I was ready. I was dying anyway."

"Oh, wow... I've heard of 'suicide by cop' but this is crazy...so then what happened?" Tim asked. "What made you change your mind? You're talking about the things you 'would have' done if you carried out your plan, but not what you're going to do now. What's changed?"

"Right," Harley smiled. "Well… two things changed. One, my health turned around. The doctors don't understand why, but this new medication I'm taking is finally working. My T-Cells are higher than they've been in years and my viral load is going back down. I might have years left. This party tonight was supposed to be for me to say goodbye to my old friends, but then I got this news and the party took on a different meaning for me. Instead of saying good-bye, I can celebrate with them. Nobody knows about any of this but the three of us, Tim. I trust you to keep it that way."

"Okay, but what's the other thing?" Tim asked. "You said there were two things that changed."

"It was that night we came to dinner at the restaurant on Castro Street…" Vanessa started.

"Yes?"

"We've been studying Arlo Montgomery for a long time, Tim. We know how he comes into town and feeds his press releases to the local papers and television stations. I even found out how the services are structured, who his helpers are, the order of the songs and the prayers. He used to pass a collection plate, but now he can charge top dollar for his extravagant shows. They're getting bigger and more professional all the time and they know how to get the crowds worked up. A Broadway producer couldn't do a more masterful job. That's where Vanessa came in. She knows people in the theatre who work for him—technical people, mostly—lighting designers, sound engineers. They helped Arlo put his shows together. They told Vanessa exactly what would happen."

"Look at this, Tim." Vanessa reached for some papers on the desk. "Here's a map of the Civic Auditorium. It shows the lighting design, how the stage will be set up, where the musicians will sit. Turn it over. There's the schedule for that evening, all the warm-up preachers and prayers and the gospel choirs and the soloists. They're building a trap door with an elevator platform so that Arlo Montgomery will ascend in a cloud of smoke from the fog machine and he'll be lit with a golden glow from directly above."

"That's right when I was going to nail him!" Harley said.

Vanessa patted her brother's knee and continued her explanation to Tim. "Arlo will appear right at midnight when the crowds are good and ready for him."

Tim turned the paper over in his hands and tried to read the fine print, but he was too stoned to focus on the details. "This is amazing, but why would these people you know want to work for him? Aren't some of your friends in the theatre gay?" Tim asked.

"Sure they are, but fewer technical people than artists. Even so, it was just another job to them. They didn't know he would be so successful. He hires them for their talents and then he takes over. It's just a job to *him*! Once they realized how much hate he was preaching, even the straight guys were willing to help me. Some of them owed me favors, after all these years." Vanessa gave Tim a coy grin.

"But you said there were two things that changed, Harley. One was that your health improved and the other had to do with Arts, where I work. What happened that night you came into the restaurant on Castro Street?"

"We discovered that you knew David Anderson. We couldn't risk you being involved. You might have been perceived as having had a motive too, don't you see?"

"I guess so..." Tim said, although he wasn't sure of anything. "So... now what happens? What do you have in mind to leave a mark on the world, Harley?"

"I'm not sure, Tim, but I'll keep fighting. When my time comes, maybe I'll leave everything to a worthwhile charity.

Bill left it to me, after all. None of this was mine in the first place." He reached for his sister's hand.

Vanessa added, "I don't need it. I just want my little brother to be happy and healthy."

Harley smiled at his sister and sighed. "And I'll go back to doing what I always did, what people in my fortunate position do, writing checks and attending fundraisers. I'll keep my hands clean and envy the guys your age who are still able to go out there and raise hell. I'll write letters and sign petitions. The pen may be mightier than the sword, but a bullet would have trumped them both. There may be a better way of fighting the likes of Arlo Montgomery than with a gun, but damnit, it sure would have felt good."

"In the meanwhile, all those phony so-called Christian bigots out there better be saying their prayers right along with me that Harley's health holds up for a long time," Vanessa said. "My prayers are real."

Tim thought about the note from Dave Anderson and the receipt in the envelope on his kitchen table. "There might be some other way. I know some guys who are planning a protest at the auditorium, but I'm not sure what they'll be able to do. I also got a tip from…" Tim almost said, "Dave," but he didn't want to complicate matters or he might be here all night. "…from an old friend who says we might not have to do anything, but just in case he disappoints me again, I'd better take a trip out to the airport tomorrow—today." He was still struggling to read the piece of paper with the map and schedule that Vanessa had given him. "Do you mind if I keep this?"

"Sure, it's only a copy and besides, all our plans are changed, now. The assassination plot, as rewarding as it would have been, is off!"

Tim folded the paper and put it in his pocket as the bedroom door opened and the noise of the party flooded in along with Artie's slurred voice, "Timmy! Are you in here? It's time for this fat old drag queen to go home. You can stay all night if you want to, but... Harley! Vanessa! What a wonderful party! Thank you so much for inviting me. I've run across people I haven't seen in years!"

"Well Artie Glamóur, we're honored that you could come," said Vanessa.

"Hold on, Artie," Tim said. "I'll come with you. I've got to work tomorrow night and I have a big day ahead. I'll hail a chariot for her majesty on Folsom Street and you can pay for it."

"Oh, honey, I'll be glad to," Artie said. "Now don't you forget to say goodnight to that darling bartender!"

Chapter 12

Tim still felt a little stoned on Saturday morning. He picked up the pill organizer beside his bed and realized he'd passed out without his bedtime meds. Maybe that was why he'd slept so well without any dreams he could remember. He could take them now, but he wasn't sure how they would affect him and he had important things to do today. Then he remembered the bartender and checked his pockets for his card. His name was Matthew and there was an e-mail address and phone number. At least he hadn't dreamed that part, but even if Tim worked up the nerve to call, he wouldn't know what to say.

He sat at the kitchen table with Dave Anderson's note in one hand and the receipt in the other. No matter how many times he looked at them and turned them over between his fingers, nothing changed. Tim flipped through the slim Saturday Chronicle until he found a brief story on the bottom of the third page about the 'Men's Gathering' at the Civic Center. So they were calling it something as innocuous as a 'gathering' now. The article mentioned the overflow crowds and that tonight was the main event, topped off by the appearance of the charismatic and inspirational Arlo Montgomery.

Tim stared at the last line of Dave's note again: *Don't lose it, but don't use it unless you absolutely have to.* Then he got to thinking… David Anderson knew Timothy Snow well enough to know that Tim didn't go around losing things. Dave knew Tim would be especially careful with something so important that it would "prove everything" in case "something happened" to Dave. Why would Dave even hint about such a thing as losing it? Dave knew Tim inside and out. Tim resented the implication until he thought about it all a little harder.

That last line sounded like a dare and then Tim got it! Dave knew that Tim's curiosity would get to him. He knew Tim would use the receipt whether he "had to" or not. He probably would have gone to the airport on Friday if Jean-Yves hadn't appeared on Thursday night to distract him, not that Tim minded the distraction. How long had Dave expected Tim to wait? Was he making his getaway right now? Could Dave Anderson have known something about Jean-Yves and included him in his plans? No. Tim was still stoned enough from Harley's pot last night to let his mind wander into paranoia. It was time to stop thinking so hard and start acting. It was time to go to the airport.

Tim boarded the #33 Ashbury at 18th and Castro and rode to the stop near the Victoria Theatre. He crossed 16th St. stepping around flower vendors and the Mexican lady selling homemade tamales from a cart. He bought a round-trip ticket and boarded the last car of the BART train to the airport. Tim rarely rode BART, but he'd heard rumors about guys cruising and even sometimes getting some action in the last car. Maybe it was Jake who mentioned it, but it was more likely Jason.

There was an Internet group where people could log on and brag about their BART adventures. Tim was always horny enough to check out the most unlikely rumors. One cute guy in glasses and a tank top might be cruising, but Tim wasn't sure. There was a young mother nursing a baby in the row between them.

Tim reached for a copy of the Contra Costa Times on the floor. The corner of the newspaper was sticky, so Tim dropped it again. It was only white chewing gum. He shuffled the pages with his feet and saw a headline about some warehouse fire and a multi-million-dollar lawsuit. He finally reached down and turned the newspaper over with his fingertips. Arlo Montgomery was on one of the inside pages, but it was an old file photo, airbrushed to give the preacher an angelic glow.

A businessman got off at Balboa Park Station and left a clean copy of the San Jose Mercury News, so Tim moved across the aisle and picked it up. He read an editorial about a religious group fighting to outlaw abortion. They'd joined forces with a group of concerned parents to keep sex education out of the schools. None of this was news to Tim, but it fired up his indignation. The same people who said gays were promiscuous always fought against gay marriage and now they were working to deny even more of their rights. Tim didn't notice someone board the train at the Colma Station and sit down behind him. The young man stared at Tim for a long time. Tim's thoughts were miles away until he glimpsed a flash of silver reflected in the window. The lights flickered off and on a couple of times as the train rolled into darkness before its approach to the South San Francisco Station.

Tim's dream flooded back to him. He was on Alcatraz on a Ferris wheel with Jason who turned into Dave Anderson and then he became the nearly naked man from the Hole in the Wall Saloon. Harley and Vanessa were in the car in front and in the seat behind him was the girl with the scar across her face. Her name was… Amy… but she reminded him of his old friend Beth… and the boy with the tattoos had a switchblade knife and he was sitting behind Tim on the BART train right now. This was no dream. "Hey, I know you!" the kid said.

Tim forced himself to turn toward the sound of the voice. "You were the guy on the streetcar the other day… the subway… under Market Street. You were staring at my girlfriend and then you got off at Castro Street and…"

"I didn't mean to…" Tim said. He was scared, but he felt his defenses rise. He hadn't meant any harm. Tim could see now that the glint of silver in the boy's hand was a fingernail file, not a knife. The kid was trying to pare some of the grease out from under his nails.

"Amy said she liked you, man," the boy said. "You reminded her of her brother."

The tension in the back of Tim's neck was released as if the weight of the world had just been lifted off his shoulders. He let out a deep breath he hadn't been aware of holding. "Your girlfriend… Amy… she reminded me of an old friend of mine, too. She seems like a nice girl."

"Her fag brother's about your age," the boy continued. "She hates when I say that, though. She was pissed off at me that I called you a fag that day on the streetcar… bad habit. It sounds like something my dad would say. Her fag brother helped raise her. He's an okay guy. He owns a chain of them beauty salons, now. He wants to pay for her to get some surgery on her face and get rid of them scars. It costs a lot of money. I told her she don't need it. She's pretty enough to me just the way she is. Whatever… it ain't *my* money. He can spend it any way he wants. Hey, I'll tell her I ran into you. This here's my stop—San Bruno. I gotta work Saturdays. My dad has a body shop and it's real busy right now. Take it easy… Seeya…"

Tim waved at the boy and noticed how clean his own hand was. Tim's father's fingernails were always lined in grease from working on cars. Then the doors closed and the BART train moved on toward the airport. Another part of his dream had come true, but things could have been much worse. At least it wasn't a knife. Maybe Amy's brother with his chain of beauty salons could even do something about her boyfriend's filthy fingernails.

Tim got on the shuttle going the wrong direction and rode all the way out to the long-term parking lots and then around the periphery of the airport to the northern terminal. He wasn't sure what he was looking for until he saw the sign: *Due to security regulations since 09/11/01, airport lockers will be out of service until further notice. Locker service is available exclusively at the Airport Travel Agency, located on the Departures/Ticketing Level of the International Terminal Main Hall.*

It was about the size of a small town post office. The man behind the counter reminded Tim of the actor Morgan Freeman when he asked, "May I help you, sir?" Tim supposed he might look suspicious in that he was wearing shorts, a T-shirt and running shoes and he wasn't carrying any luggage.

"I hope so." Tim gave the man a weak smile. "A friend of mine checked something here and he asked me to pick it up for him. Here's the receipt."

The man disappeared behind a panel and came back out a moment later with a manila envelope, but he didn't hand it to Tim. "This was checked on Tuesday. Today is Saturday. Your friend only paid for two days."

"He ran into some… ah… trouble," Tim said, trying to think of a plausible story. "He's sick. I'm sure he didn't expect it to take so long to get it back. How much does he… do I owe you?"

"It's three dollars a day. He paid for two days, so that comes to six more dollars."

Now that Tim had the package in his hand he hardly knew what to do with it. He felt like he needed to set it down before it burned his fingers. He found the nearest Men's room and locked himself inside one of the stalls. When he opened the envelope and looked at the contents Tim felt sick. Yes, this could bring Arlo Montgomery down instead of Harley's bullet, but it wouldn't be nearly as clean and quick.

The first pictures showed Arlo with several naked boys and young men. They were splashing and diving in a watering hole somewhere in the woods. They might have been taken with a telephoto lens without Arlo Montgomery even knowing about them. As Tim paged through the pile they became more incriminating and much more explicit.

The bathroom stalls on either side of Tim's were empty and the light from the ceiling shone in. Tim held the pictures down by the floor to study them better. Judging from the furnishings, these must have been in hotel rooms. Why had Arlo Montgomery allowed these pictures to be taken? There were beer cans and liquor bottles on the bedside tables. Some of the boys were tied up and most of them looked like they were either asleep or in a stupor. Tim remembered pictures of prisoner abuse at Abu Ghraib. Maybe Arlo thought of them as trophies, showing off his conquests in some sick way. Or did Dave Anderson take them from a hiding place? No, Dave was in a few of the pictures, too and he appeared to be taking an active part. He still could have set up the camera... but Tim might never know. And the thing that upset Tim most was that some of the boys were so young—even younger than Tim was when he and Dave first met.

Tim had to talk to someone right away. He called the restaurant to get Patrick's cell phone number, but regretted it when Artie answered. He would have to deal with Artie's questions sooner or later, but at least he got the number and

Artie became distracted by a delivery coming in the door, so he let Tim off the hook for the time being. Patrick was thrilled by the news about the photographs and told Tim to meet him and Barry on the double. They agreed to wait for him at the Civic Center BART station and they would come up with a plan.

Tim was relieved to have told someone—anyone—about the pictures, but he was still reeling at the shock of finding them. Maybe he should have called Harley Wagner first. Maybe he should have called the police. He wished his Aunt Ruth was close by, if only to talk things over. He wouldn't want her to actually see the pictures. All he could do now was trust Patrick and his friend. Tim headed toward the BART shuttle and stared at the overhead map, trying to figure out which direction to go. He didn't want to take another tour of the long-term parking lots. Tim thought about the envelope he held in his hands and went inside another Men's room. This time he had to wait for a stall to empty. He locked himself inside, tore up every picture that showed Dave Anderson's face and flushed them down the toilet. Then he found his way to a BART train bound for San Francisco.

Chapter 13

"Patrick, are you sure you know what you're doing?" Tim asked. The three of them had ridden the F-Line streetcar from the Civic Center BART station down Market Street to the nearest copy store. Barry was biting the end off a glue stick while Patrick wielded a pair of scissors.

"Don't worry, Tim," Patrick said. "Barry was an art major at City College."

"These pictures are awesome, man. We'll make a collage of the most incriminating ones and run off a ton of them."

Barry was having fun with the project, but Tim still had his doubts. "Shouldn't we just call the police right now? Some of those boys have to be minors. I have to work tonight, but I want to know exactly what happens when Arlo Montgomery's supporters see these pictures."

"You can leave everything to us, Tim," Patrick said. "A bunch of our guys went down there in suits and ties earlier this week to volunteer. They didn't need all of us, but they will tonight because it's sold out. Tonight all the VIPs will show up and they can use more ushers. One section down in front is reserved for well-known politicians, some actors and a few big names in sports, but the big-shots don't want to sit through all the warm-up acts. Just wait until they see their programs with something extra that we've tucked inside."

"That reminds me… that old lady Vanessa gave me a map we can use if we need it." Tim searched through the bottom of his pack until he found it. "Here, it shows the floor plan of the Civic Auditorium, the stage set-up, the lighting design, special effects devices and the schedule of events is on the back. Arlo is supposed to appear at midnight, after the crowds are all warmed up for him. We should make extra copies of this too."

"Why not call in sick to work so you can join us from the beginning?" Barry said.

"I can't! You don't know Artie," Tim said. "I promised him a week ago that I'd work tonight."

"Come down to the Civic Center as soon as you get off, then," Patrick said. "There won't be anybody in the Castro tonight, anyway. Everybody that's not picketing outside the Bill Graham Auditorium will be dancing all night at the Moscone Center. I don't even know why they're bothering to open the restaurant."

"I don't either, but I've gotta go get ready," Tim said. "I'll come down and look for you the minute I get off work. If anything happens before I get there, call me at the restaurant." This was one of the rare times that Tim wished he owned a cell phone, but he complained about them so much that he was too stubborn to break down and get one.

He was sure that the hours at work would drag by while all the excitement was happening somewhere else. Once inside the front gate on Collingwood, he opened his mailbox to find a PG&E bill, an advertisement for a new gay travel agency, a supermarket flyer and a thin blue envelope with a San Diego postmark, but no return address. Tim's name and address were printed in block letters across the front. He sat down on the front steps and tore it open.

Dear Tim—I trust by now you have been to the airport. I wonder how long you waited and I wish I could have seen the look on your face. I couldn't let Arlo continue his crusade, but I wasn't brave enough to stop him directly. As far as he knows right now I'm just another suicide off the Golden Gate Bridge. Let him think so. Whatever happens will be too good for him. It was great to see you, Tim. I'm glad you're doing well. I won't flatter myself that you'd ever want to find me, but the authorities won't be able to either. I have a new passport and all the money I will ever need, thanks to the devout and pious men who wanted to be saved from the clutches of sin. What fools! Arlo was a fool, too, for giving me access to the bank accounts. He'll need more than a public defender now, but that's all he'll be able to afford. I hear that Mexico is hot this time of year, but I think I'll start there. I don't mind hot weather and I've heard that the boys down south of the border come sexy and cheap. Take care of yourself, Tim—Dave

Tim read the letter twice before he stood up from his front steps and walked to his front door. He was tempted again to call the police, but it wouldn't do any good. David Anderson was long gone by now and he would have to live with his conscience. Tim just wanted to wash his hands of the whole mess, but all he could do was let the plan go forward. He turned the key and noticed a note under his door. It was written on a brown paper grocery bag in magic marker:

Tim—A delivery came for you this afternoon. Come upstairs as soon as you get home—Teresa.

Tim tucked the letter from Dave with his other note next to the toaster. He could hardly wait to take a long hot shower, but he at least washed his hands and face before he dashed upstairs to knock on Teresa's door. She answered with tears in her eyes and a catch in her voice. "Come on in, honey. Something came for you about an hour ago and they rang my bell by mistake."

"What's the matter, Teresa? Are you crying? Wait a minute… are you drunk?"

"Are you kidding?" she replied as her way of answering. "Who wouldn't be? Tony said he was expecting an important phone call and he was in the shower when his cell phone went off, so I answered it."

"Who was it?"

"It was his goddamn wife!" Teresa screamed. "She called to tell him she was going into labor! I didn't even know the bastard was married!"

"What did you do?"

"I threw the phone in the shower at him and then I threw his clothes out the front window onto the sidewalk. Then I made myself a stiff drink and I sat down and drank it and then I made another one as soon as he left. If I ever see him again, I'll kill him! Do you want a cocktail, Tim?"

"No thanks, Teresa, I've got to get ready for work," Tim said holding up her hand-written note. "What was it that came for me?"

"Oh, yeah…" she pointed toward the kitchen. "There's a couple of dozen long-stemmed roses in a crystal vase. There's a card with them. You'd better take them home before I knock them over. It's lucky they arrived after that bastard was gone or I would have broken that vase over his head! He ran off with one of my best towels, too!"

"I'm really sorry, Teresa, but I've got to get ready for work. Will you be all right?"

"Oh sure, hon… you go on."

Tim carried the heavy vase and his card down the stairs and set the flowers on his own kitchen table. He wondered whether Dave had bought these with some of the money he'd embezzled from Arlo Montgomery. Tim tore open the card and saw that it was from Corey.

> *Dear Tim— Well, I'm back to my everyday rut. I have a huge reading list to finish up before my next semester starts, but I wanted to let you know I've been thinking of you. I wish I could be with you under that big mirror ball on Saturday night, although I'd rather be with you someplace more private. My friends are glad to see me back, of course, but that's what friends are for, I guess. I don't know how to thank you for showing me around. You're a great guy and you really made my visit special. If you ever get to this part of the country be sure to look me up. In the meantime, I'll see you in my dreams. I hope you like roses. I'm sending them with lots of big wet sloppy kisses —Corey.*
>
> *p.s.— I've enclosed a picture of the two of us at that beach in San Francisco when we interrupted you trying to read. I can't say that I'm sorry. Donald and Jerry had their camera along and one of them snapped it. I already have a copy on my refrigerator. It's the first of my collection of memories and I'm sure it will always be one of my favorites.*

Tim moved the roses to his bedside table and set the note there, too. He could fall asleep to their fragrance for as long as they lasted and remember his time with Corey. It was funny that Corey's note mentioned dreams. Tim couldn't remember if he'd told Corey that his dreams had a way of coming true ever since he was a boy.

Tim inhaled a big whiff of the flowers and made room for the photograph on his refrigerator. Corey was a nice kid. Tim would have to stop ignoring guys that were younger than him. It had gotten to be a bad habit, but one he knew he could break if he tried.

Tim started to get undressed for the shower, but clicked on his e-mail to see a dozen new messages. The only important one was from his Aunt Ruth.

Dear Tim— I've done it! I made the reservations and bought my tickets. My flight arrives on the last Friday of this month at 10:45am. I'll get a cab from the airport and hope they can find Collingwood Street. If I tell the driver you live in the Castro that will be a good place to start looking. I'll only stay with you for the first three nights and then check into a hotel. You know what the Chinese say about fish and house guests. I've cancelled the papers and arranged for my neighbor lady Erna to feed Bartholomew and take care of the litter box, water my plants and bring in the mail. The lawn sprinklers are on a timer and I've paid that sweet boy named Kyle who lives down the street with his grandparents to keep up the mowing. He does it anyway so he has a key to the shed. I guess you didn't hear any more from Dave Anderson. It's just as well. I feel sorry for his poor wife Nancy, but I'm not going to run all the way over to the Mall of America just to have another glass of wine at the Napa Valley Grille. I don't mind some clever dish with the girls, but if what you say turns out to be true then he's really not coming back to her and that falls beyond the category of harmless gossip. I'd hate to have to give anyone such bad news. I can't think of anything else right now but to say how excited I am to see you soon and I can't wait to catch up.   Much love, Aunt Ruth

Tim wondered whether he should hit "reply" and tell his Aunt Ruth about the pictures Dave left him and what was going to happen tonight. If she assumed that Tim hadn't heard any more from his old track coach, it might be better to leave it that way. Whatever happened tonight, she would probably hear it on the news. He turned off the computer and stripped off the last of his clothes. The shower felt good and there was decent water pressure for a change. He let it beat down on him until it started running cold. Between working at Arts and whatever happened at the Civic Center, not to mention the throngs of people going to the Moscone Center party, it was bound to be a very long night in San Francisco.

The waiters at Arts didn't have uniforms and Artie wasn't a stickler about what they wore as long as they looked neat and clean. He complained each time Jake had an ear or eyebrow pierced in another spot, but Artie and Arturo were more concerned that the customers were comfortable. On Saturday when Tim left for work, he wore a crisp white dress shirt and stuck a necktie in his pocket for later. He knew he'd be too late to get inside Bill Graham Auditorium with the other volunteers, but he wanted to blend in as best he could and the sooner he got to the Civic Center the better. He was nervous that something would go wrong to foil Patrick's plan. The more he thought about the pictures of Arlo Montgomery with those young men and boys, the more he wished he had taken them to the police or to the newspapers.

Arturo had given most of the staff the night off with so much happening around town, but Saturday night started out busy. Even some of the guys who were headed to the Moscone Center party were sensible enough to eat before going out. Artie speculated that the early diners were old enough to remember Sylvester and therefore less apt to do "whatever the kids snort up their noses nowadays to stay up dancing all night," in Arturo's words.

As the only waiter, Tim had plenty to do. Even though half the tables were empty, the diners who did come in were spread out all over the room. With Artie alone behind the bar, it took longer than usual to get drinks. Even Jorge, the dishwasher and part-time busboy, took the night off for a rock concert at the Warfield with his newest girlfriend. No one at Arts had ever heard of the band, but that was no surprise.

The first part of the shift Artie talked about nothing but Harley's party. "I danced with Carol Doda!" he told everyone who sat down at the bar. Most of the customers knew who Carol Doda was and if they encouraged him Artie would regale them with stories of everyone else who was at the party, always returning to tales of the *good old days* in North Beach.

Tim was glad to see Artie happy, but when he needed to order drinks he wished Jason or Patrick were behind the bar. At one point he stepped into the kitchen to pick up a dinner order and Arturo asked how things were going out front.

"It's busier than I expected, Arturo," Tim said. "I think we could have used two waiters and two bartenders after all, but we'll get by."

"I thought you were past pining over Jason, Tim," Arturo said frowning.

"That is not what I meant, Arturo!" Corey and Jean-Yves had helped take his mind off Jason. "I was talking about business."

"You know, Tim... Jason cares for you very much," Arturo said. "He's just not ready to settle down right now. You'll meet someone when the time is right. Falling in love has more to do with being in the right place at the right time than almost anything else. I'm convinced of that."

"Oh, Arturo... I know you only mean the best for me, but... Are these plates ready?" Tim didn't want to discuss it.

"Yes, run along before they get cold."

As the evening wore on, Artie told everyone who would listen all about the party on Clementina Street, but gradually shifted his thoughts to the present day. Tim kept busy enough not to have time for a lot of questions, but whenever there was a lull, Artie wanted to know what his sudden friendship with Patrick was all about. "I didn't think you even liked Patrick, Tim. I know he gets carried away with his causes, but he means well, you know."

"I have nothing against causes," Tim protested, although he did in some cases. People who preached to their friends and co-workers about anything, whether they were reformed smokers, born-again Christians, over-zealous environmentalists or gay rights activists—they all made Tim uncomfortable. "It's just a Minnesota thing."

"What were you doing at the airport this afternoon, Tim?" Artie finally put it to him so directly that Tim didn't know how to avoid the truth. He didn't want to explain Patrick's plan before he knew if it would be successful. Something else occurred to Tim, too. Harley and Vanessa had said they found out about Dave Anderson's connection with Tim when they came to Arts, but Tim hadn't been the one to tell them.

"Artie, did you ever hear of a guy named David Anderson?"

"Sure, Vanessa and Harley were talking about him the other night when they were in for dinner. Why do you ask?" Artie could be just as aggravating as anyone.

"What do you mean, Artie?" Tim demanded. "What did they say about Dave Anderson? Did they ask about him in connection with me?"

"They asked me if I'd ever heard of him," Artie admitted.

"And… what did you tell them? *Had* you ever heard of him?"

"Tim… you mentioned him yourself a long time ago."

"I never told you about Dave Anderson. I would have remembered something like that."

"No, but you must have told Jason about him. Arturo and I ran into you and Jason one day when you were both off work. It was a beautiful morning and he had the top down on the Thunderbird. I think he was picking you up to go to the beach. Jason was teasing you about something and you told him to shut up because he sounded just like Dave Anderson. You two were just horsing around, already smoking a joint in the driveway on Collingwood—we could smell it before we got downstairs to the gate. Arturo and I were so shocked to hear the name that I asked how you knew him. You tried to clam up pretty quick, but we got the gist."

"I don't understand," Tim said. "Jason and I went to the beach lots of times, but why would you remember that day? How could you know Dave Anderson?"

"Oh, we didn't—not *that* Dave Anderson. It's a common name. We knew another Dave Anderson in Viet Nam, that's all. He was the meanest son of a bitch you'd ever want to meet. That was why I remembered, but even if he were alive, he'd be at least sixty by now and I know he's dead. I watched him die and I'm almost ashamed to say I didn't feel bad about it. I can't recall exactly how his name came up the other night, but I think Vanessa asked me. The Chronicle was sitting on the bar and there had been those pictures about the preacher coming to town, you know. We got to talking and I told her yes, that you and I both knew guys named David Anderson, but that was a long time ago. We were having such a nice time talking about show business that I didn't want to even think about Vietnam. I told her I didn't think you'd want to talk about Dave Anderson either, but he was someone in your past when you were a kid in Minnesota. So… what were you doing at the airport?"

Tim was spared from giving a direct answer when his second floor neighbors from Collingwood Street, Ben and Jane Larson, came in with their daughter Sarah. "Hi, Artie!" Jane called from the front door as Ben picked up his little girl and set her on a barstool. "Are you serving straight people here tonight?"

"Jane... Ben! Hello, Sarah. How's my little cutie tonight? Yes, come in and sit down. We're serving anyone with cash or credit," Artie said.

"The neighborhood seems kind of quiet for a Saturday," Jane said.

"We had a good rush earlier," Artie explained. "Most of the boys have gone off to the big dance down at the Moscone Center. The rest of the evening looks like it will be straights and lesbians."

"Can you say hi to Artie, Sarah?" Ben asked his daughter. "You know Tim who lives downstairs from us, don't you? This is where Tim and Artie work."

The little girl said hi, but was more interested in staring at the framed photographs of local celebrities on the wall behind the bar. "Who's that man, Mommy? I think I saw him on TV. Who is the pretty blonde lady?"

"That's Robin Williams," said Tim as he came up behind the little girl. "Do you get *TV Land* on cable? He was on *Mork and Mindy*. The blonde lady is Sharon Stone. She used to live here in town, but I think she moved away."

"Even Viv took off early tonight, but I don't think she's going dancing. She's got a new gentleman friend—at her age! He's a big old cowboy," Artie said. "Jason is tending bar down at the dance party and Patrick is... Tim! You never did tell me about Patrick. What's going on with you and him?"

"I'd like a Shirley Temple and a hamburger, please," Sarah blurted out.

"Maybe we could all sit down at a table first and look at the menu?" Jane suggested.

"Right this way," said Tim, averting Artie's questions again.

It was nearly eleven when the last of Tim's tables finished eating, but they were still lingering over coffee, a twenty-something straight couple oblivious to anyone but each other. Arturo came out of the kitchen and pronounced it closed. When he saw Tim still there, he asked him if he'd like to cut out. "There's no sense in hanging around for one table, Tim. Have they paid their check? If those love birds want more coffee, they can get it themselves."

"Thanks, Arturo," Tim said. "I might be able to catch up with some friends if I hurry." Tim grabbed his jacket and nearly made it to the door when Artie tried to question him again, but he called back over his shoulder, "I promise I'll tell you all about it tomorrow, Artie. I've gotta go!"

Chapter 14

Tim stepped out onto Castro Street and walked north toward the corner of 18th until he could flag a cab going his direction. "Civic Center, please," he said to the driver, a middle-aged man with a long gray ponytail.

"Don't you mean the Moscone Center?" The driver assumed that Tim was another gay tourist. "That's where the big dance party's happening. You don't want to go near the Civic Center. It's a mess!"

"No, I mean the Civic Center. I live here. That's where I'm going. What do you mean, it's a mess?"

"I haven't seen so many cops down there since the riots on the night of the Dan White verdict, but I reckon you're too young to remember any of that…"

If Tim hadn't noticed the ponytail and gold hoop earring, the cab driver also had elaborate tattoos snaking up both arms from the wrists past his well-developed biceps. He had to be at least in his late fifties, but he still oozed a comfortable sensuality that bordered on downright sexiness. "You mean you were actually here for the gay riots?" Tim wondered if the driver knew Harley Wagner.

"Hell, yeah! 1979… I helped turn over the first police car at the corner of Grove and Polk and we used my Zippo lighter to torch it! This is the same lighter right here! I should bring it to that antiques roadshow on TV and tell them the story. It might be worth a lot of money by now. The first police car… whoosh!" He snapped the lighter open and lit a small clay pipe. Tim soon caught a whiff of pot and sat back in his seat as the driver accelerated down Market Street.

"Wanna hit?"

"Sure, man…thanks!" Tim pulled himself forward with both hands on the back of the front seat before the light changed to green at Sanchez and he was thrown back again.

"That mutha-fucka killed Harvey Milk and George Moscone and they gave him a slap on the wrist! I grew up in New York, but I been here since '67—'Summer of Love,' man." The driver still had a trace of a Brooklyn accent and Tim realized that this guy, though he might not be someone Tim would even notice in a Castro Street bar, was still hot! It gave him hope for a long life to a ripe old age in San Francisco.

The driver continued, "That was when Dianne Feinstein was mayor and she acted like we should all just be good little boys and go home and play nice. There was nothing but sheer rage coming out of all of us. By the time of the Dan White verdict, it was a decade after the drag queens in New York had fought back at Stonewall and we'd had some minor battles under our belts already, but this one was our turn. It was still a few years before AIDS hit, before Feinstein shut down the bathhouses, when we had to re-shift the focus to burying our dead."

"Wow!" Tim felt like a kid in front of his favorite cartoon show on a Saturday morning. Although he was never fond of history in books in school, he loved hearing real people tell about the times they'd lived through that he'd missed out on. "I wish I could have been here for the riots."

"It was really something, man... and then later that night the cops swept down Castro Street and bashed heads at the Elephant Walk. That's where that bar called Harvey's is now, right on the corner of 18th and Castro. The cops had no business coming down here... you want I should turn north on Franklin and try to get up closer on Grove Street? The television crews are blocking a lot of the area, not to mention the security and the limousines for all the big-shots."

"No, that's okay. Stay on Market Street," Tim said. "The corner of 9th is fine." Part of Tim wished he could have been there in 1979, but he also noticed searchlights streaking across the sky a few blocks off to his right. The party at the Moscone Center would be getting into full swing and Tim wished he could be there, too. Jason would be tending bar and no doubt have his shirt off by now, raking in the tips. Jean-Yves would be there, too. Tim had a wicked desire to find out where Jason was working and take Jean-Yves right up to that bar to order drinks and show him off. Nah... it was a childish fantasy... first things first... he had to find Patrick.

Tim over-tipped the driver, but it was worth it to meet someone besides Harley Wagner who had been in San Francisco the night of the White Night riots. That was two people in one week and it put Tim in the mood for whatever was about to go down. He looked at his watch. It was a few minutes past 11:30. He might still make it there in time to see what was going to happen. Tim ran across Market, then Larkin at Hayes and he came around the East side of the Civic Auditorium. He hadn't been here since the Pride Celebration after the gay parade and that was during daylight hours. Now it was night and a blanket of fog had come in, but Tim was too excited to feel the cold.

He heard the crackle of police walkie-talkies and paramedics on distant radios. Tim noticed a cluster of official vehicles in front of the main library and the red taillights of chartered busses across the plaza on McAllister Street. Rounding the corner onto Grove Street, his first sight was a group of boys in white shirts and ties kneeling in a circle. The oldest of them was maybe in his early twenties. Some were really cute, Tim thought, and that led to thoughts of Corey again and Tim fought off feeling horny. Then he got close enough to realize the boys were on their knees in a circle because they were praying. Tim could smell their cheap aftershave and noticed the acne on the back of one boy's neck. They reminded him of the young Mormons that he sometimes saw on MUNI busses wearing their suits with nametags and trying to strike up conversations with souls that needed saving.

Aside from the men who attended the rally, Arlo Montgomery had drawn a wide array of onlookers, press and protesters of every persuasion from pro-Israel and anti-gay picketers to Green Party members and advocates for the homeless and the disabled. A couple of the Sisters of Perpetual Indulgence dressed in red, white and blue were sitting down next to their glittering high heeled shoes and rubbing their tired feet. Tim saw a large flash of something white come sailing through the air and land in the middle of the prayer group, but not before it sliced a deep cut in the ear of one of the smaller kids. Blood poured down the boy's white shirt and splattered across his clip-on necktie. The weapon was only a pasteboard sign on a stick. It said something about the wages of sin. Tim thought the little boy's blood was splattered across the sign, but it was red paint from an artist's depiction of hellfire lit by the spinning red light of a nearby fire truck.

The little boy put his hands to the sides of his head and yelled, "Ouch! I'm bleeding!" Tears rolled down his cheeks and mixed with the blood.

Tim helped the poor kid stand up while the others rejoined hands and went on praying. They seemed more intent on re-closing their circle with their backs to the world than stopping to care for the injured boy. Tim wondered what the kid was doing out there in the first place. "Come on!" Tim yelled. He pulled a handkerchief out of his pocket to put pressure on the boy's ear. "Come on! Come with me. There's an ambulance on the corner. I'll take you over there and they can patch you up. What's your name?"

"Luke… who are you?"

"My name is Tim. Where are you from?"

"Minnesota," the boy said. He looked dazed and scared, but he allowed Tim to lead him away. "It's my first time in Frisco."

"No kidding! I'm from Minnesota, too!"

"Oh, yeah? My dad's a preacher and we came out here on an old school bus. Him and me and my brothers follow Pastor Montgomery all over the place. Sometimes we go camping and we sleep in the bus and sometimes he lets some of us stay in his hotel room with him, but not me, not yet… he says I'm too little. The twins over there are John and Joseph. They just turned seventeen. They're Pastor Montgomery's favorites. We used to pass the collection plates, but now they sell tickets in advance and his men find us odd jobs to do. Tonight we handed out programs but everyone's inside now so we're finished."

"Here's the ambulance," Tim said. "These people will patch you up."

"Hey, thanks a lot, mister…"

"Don't mention it… but think of me next time you're praying for the sinners… or against us. I'm one of them.

I'm gay." The paramedics pulled the boy into an ambulance before Tim could tell whether he'd heard Tim's last words, but he felt good for having said them. Now he wanted to find Patrick and Barry, but the scene outside was chaotic. Police were lined up with their backs to the auditorium and an even larger group of young dykes with signs and whistles taunted them from the opposite side of Grove Street.

"Hey-Hey! Ho-Ho! Homophobia's got to go!" they shouted, following the lead of the big leather-clad one with a bullhorn. Tim thought they needed a catchier chant, but he couldn't think of any at the moment. It seemed like more testosterone was coming from the line of lesbians protesting than from all the armed policemen, many of whom looked bored.

The entrances to the auditorium were closed and blocked by a pair of security guards in front of each doorway. The audience must all be in their seats by now, even the VIP section. Tim tied his necktie as he walked behind the row of police. He wanted to look like he could have been one of the ushers who just stepped outside for some fresh air or maybe a cigarette break. Did any of the guys who followed Arlo Montgomery smoke cigarettes, Tim wondered? He wished he had a joint about now.

"Hey Tim! Over here!" Patrick and Barry yelled at him. Barry had his heavy backpack on his shoulders.

"What's going on, you guys? I got here as fast as I could." Tim could see that things hadn't gone as planned.

"They wouldn't let us inside. They said they had enough ushers. The only guys from our group that got in were the ones who were here last night and they were assigned to sections way up high in the balconies. I think Arlo's people got suspicious of us."

"Maybe it's because you're carrying that huge backpack, Barry?"

"These damned flyers weigh a ton, but I think Arlo's henchmen are really nervous because your buddy Dave Anderson didn't turn up."

"Where are all the gay protesters?" Tim asked. "It looks like everyone out here except that bunch of dykes has another agenda."

"There were a ton of 'em earlier, but most of the guys left once Arlo's audience was all inside and the thing started," Barry said. "You'll see them later on the news."

"They probably went to the Moscone Center," Patrick said. "But don't worry. Barry and I faxed a copy of our collage to the Mayor's Office, especially to his gay liaison, and another one to the chief of police."

"And every member of the board of supervisors, the fire department, all the newspapers... if Patrick hadn't stopped me I would have sent one to the SPCA!" Barry said. "Even Michael Jackson's lawyers would have a hard time defending Montgomery with those photographs."

"Then why aren't the police doing something about it?" Tim frowned and scratched his head. "We've got to find a way inside there. That's all there is to it. Where's that map? There's gotta be a side door someplace. Come on!"

They headed west between guards on their left and the line of police on their right. "Hey Tim! What's up?" Tim turned toward the sound of the voice and recognized a man who was an occasional customer at Arts. He was in a uniform and guarding the last set of doors with a butch-looking woman.

"Wayne Friday, what are you doing here?" Tim asked.

"We were hired to do security. What does it look like? We're better off out here than inside where we can hear all their antigay crap. This is my partner Birdie Fuller. Birdie, this is Tim. He works at one of my favorite restaurants in town."

Tim quickly introduced his friends. "We've got to get inside, Wayne."

"But the protest is going on out here," Birdie said. "You're not exactly dressed like them, though. You guys look like you're on your way to Sunday school."

Tim motioned for Barry to turn around so that he could open his backpack and pull out one of the flyers. "Here... look at this... can you let us in?"

"Holy shhhhh..." Wayne started to say.

"No, we can't let anybody in!" Birdie cut him off, but Wayne already had the door open. Birdie took one look at the flyer and let out a whistle before she handed it back to Tim and stood back to let the three of them pass.

"Whoa! Wait a minute!" Tim said. "I just realized something. I know who two of these kids in the pictures are. They're right over there, the blonde twins. Their names are Joseph and John. I helped their little brother Luke into an ambulance a few minutes ago. Give me that backpack, Barry. You two guys go over to where all those boys are kneeling in a circle. Find these two—Joseph and John—tell them they have to come right away. Make up something, anything, just go get them and meet me backstage."

Tim thought he'd studied the map well enough to find his way to a side door near the stage, but he got turned around and stopped to find the map again and have another look. The hallways were set up with tables selling religious books and literature, T-shirts, caps and flag lapel pins, music CDs and DVDs of Arlo Montgomery's sermons. Tim ran down the hallway and heard footsteps in close pursuit. "Where do you think you're going?"

Tim could hear a tenor soloist in the middle of a rousing gospel song and the string section of musicians sounded like they were directly above his head when two uniformed SFPD officers caught up with him. He dropped Barry's heavy pack and thought about making a run for it, but he'd come too close to give up their plan now. Tim reached inside and pulled out a handful of the flyers. He handed them to the policemen and watched for their reaction.

"We already saw these down at the station. That's why we're here, to see about this whole mess with the preacher, but who are you?" The policemen glared at Tim.

"Who are *all* of you? What are you doing here? No one is allowed backstage except my staff. Where are my bodyguards?" Arlo Montgomery's voice was powerful, but his stature was far less imposing than Tim expected. Even in the semi-darkness his make-up showed and he appeared to be a gaunt little man swallowed up in his velvet robes.

"We're here from the San Francisco Police Department investigating a tip regarding sexual misconduct with juveniles. Those of your bodyguards who were unwilling to co-operate have already been taken into custody."

"It's a lie! All of it! Dave Anderson put you up to this, didn't he! He embezzled my money and now he's trying to cover his tracks!"

"This is the first I've heard the name, but we'll check him out too. Here's what you ought to be more concerned about, Reverend." The policeman thrust one of the flyers in Arlo Montgomery's face.

"You don't believe that filth, do you? Anybody can doctor up a photograph nowadays."

"The originals are in the bottom of this bag," Tim said and started digging for them.

"They're fakes! Forgeries!"

"No, they're not, *Reverend* Arlo!" It was Joseph, one of the blonde twins. He and his brother John crowded into the low-ceilinged space beneath the stage with Barry and Patrick right behind them.

"You boys keep your mouths shut!"

"But you always said you liked our mouths, *Pastor* Montgomery," John smirked. "You said our mouths were just as good as…"

"Shut up! It's blasphemy!"

"But he didn't like our mouths as much as he liked some other things…" John's twin brother Joseph snarled his words like a knife plunging deeper and they all watched Arlo Montgomery cringe.

The audience cheered for the gospel singer and the timpanist started a deep bass drum roll followed by a trumpet fanfare. Smoke started billowing from the fog machine. Tim shouted to Patrick and Barry, "Come on, you guys! We've got work to do!"

They found a set of wooden stairs that led up to the stage behind the drummer. They ran through the wings until they reached the main floor in front of the audience. Tim looked up to see that every seat in the cavernous auditorium was full now. Harley had been right about the handicapped section. It was front and center, flanked with three rows of cushioned armchairs on either side. Tim recognized the faces of men in the audience that he'd only seen on television or in the newspapers. There was a former governor, at least a dozen Republican congressmen from several western states, a former mayor and chief of police and even a few minor movie stars.

Tim started handing out flyers row by row, but the audience was so focused on the stage that most people took one and passed the rest along the row without looking down to see what they held in their hands. Tim glanced at his watch. It was midnight and the fog machine kicked into high gear right on schedule as the platform rose in the center of the stage. The smoke dissipated enough for Arlo Montgomery to appear where he was supposed to, but he was sputtering obscenities that were broadcast from his lapel microphone through the sound system. And he was wearing handcuffs, flanked on either side by one of San Francisco's finest.

Patrick and Barry had spread out to work the sides of the room and the flyers swept through the crowd like bad drugs at a rock concert. Instead of the usual chorus of *Amen*s and cheers that he was used to, Arlo Montgomery was pelted with boos and the shouting of words rarely heard at a Christian gathering. Then they started throwing things—plastic water bottles, crumpled programs and food wrappers. The policemen hustled Arlo toward the brass section and down the back steps off the stage, but not before one overzealous homophobe in the audience threw his Bible at him. It came spinning through the air as if in slow motion and landed with a thud across the back of the reverend's lacquered hair.

Twenty minutes later Tim managed to find his cohorts out in front on Grove Street. They headed north across the Civic Center Plaza behind a small group of gay guys with signs reading: BIGOTS GO HOME! They had to go out of their way to escape the rush of angry crowds that were still pouring out of the building. Tim smelled freshly mown lawns and thought he detected a trace of teargas amid the marijuana smoke of another group of protesters. Their signs read: MARIJUANA IS MEDICINE! and SAFE ACCESS NOW!

Tim and Barry and Patrick were still laughing as they sat down to catch their breath on the steps of City Hall. They watched the charter buses on McAllister Street begin to start up and get ready to pull away.

"You know, it's true what they always say—a picture is worth a thousand words!" Patrick grinned.

"It's a good thing for him, too, "Barry said. "He'll be safer in jail than out here with all those right-wing nut cases after they found out he was screwing around with young boys. They would have lynched him from the flagpole right in front of City Hall!"

"Yeah, I suppose you're right," Tim agreed, "but I still don't know why Dave left me those pictures. There must have been some other way to stop him."

Patrick said, "If it weren't for the photographs, no one would have believed it. They would have thought it was all a lie and he was being persecuted. Arlo Montgomery's followers would have made him into a martyr. I mean… it's not like he was a priest. He didn't have the whole Catholic Church hierarchy behind him. It took those pictures to make them see the truth and admit to themselves that they'd been duped."

Barry added, "Maybe next time they won't be so quick to follow every fake that comes along offering salvation. Arlo might have scammed millions, but I don't know what he'll do now. Even if he claimed he was on drugs and went into *rehab* it's going to cost him all the money he has and then some. Just think of the lawyers' fees if he's ever going to get out of a long prison term."

"According to Dave, I don't think he has the money," Tim said. "He might be able to use whatever profit they took in tonight, but Dave ran off with the rest. I probably shouldn't have torn up the pictures with Dave in them, but I didn't want to be reminded. That's another thing I don't understand… why Dave didn't destroy them first."

"Maybe he was testing you, Tim," Patrick said.

"Yeah, maybe… and maybe I'll never know for sure." Tim had sat down beside Patrick and Barry and put his head in his hands. He felt a mix of emotions, but most of all he was relieved that it was all over.

A black stretch limousine rounded the corner from McAllister and crept down Polk Street toward the main steps of City Hall. "I wonder what they're still doing out here," Tim said. "I thought all the rich big-shots were the first ones to flee the scene."

The three of them started walking toward Market Street. "Do you want to catch a cab back to the Castro together, maybe have a beer or something to celebrate?" Barry asked. "We've got plenty of time to make last call somewhere."

"I thought you'd be going to the Moscone Center, Tim," Patrick said.

"Nah," Tim said. "I would have liked to, but I've got to work the brunch shift with you and Artie tomorrow morning. Besides, do you know what those tickets cost? And they're twice as much at the door as they were in advance."

The limousine crept to a stop beside them and one of the tinted rear windows slid open a few inches, but they couldn't see inside. A deep voice shouted, "Tim! Tim Snow! Come here! We've been looking for you."

Tim felt a chill down his spine and hurried his pace. "Come on you guys! Let's get out of here!" Tim was sure that Dave Anderson was out of the country by now and they had all witnessed Arlo Montgomery being hauled away. Who could still be out here wanting to get even with him? Who would dare try anything? The police were nearby and the TV crews and cameramen were still packing up their gear. Tim and Patrick and Barry got as far as the statue of Abraham Lincoln when the limo caught up to them again and pulled over to the curb.

The driver got out and walked around the front toward them. Tim thought of Corey for a moment. Was this the kind of fear he lived with every day? Hell, at least Corey had bodyguards. All Tim had were these couple of guys in their thrift-store suits posing as homophobic conservatives for one night. They didn't look very tough right now with their neckties undone and their dress shirts unbuttoned halfway. "Holy shit!" Tim said. "Now what do we do?" He wondered if they should try to make a run for the nearest police car or just let out a yell and hope someone heard them.

Chapter 15

As the limousine window glided all the way down they could smell a whiff of marijuana smoke and then they heard a tenor voice singing, "*You make me feel… mighty real*" to a disco beat. Another voice—that of a woman—said, "Timothy Snow! I'm so glad we found you. We went by the restaurant, but Artie and Arturo told us you'd already left."

Tim breathed a sigh of relief. He was only being paranoid and he hadn't even smoked any pot since the single toke off that cab-driver's pipe. Harley Wagner and Vanessa Caen were in the back of the limousine. The chauffer had only gotten out to come around and open the door for him.

"Harley, Vanessa…what are you doing out here? You scared me to death!" Tim sputtered. "What's with this limo, anyway?"

"It's Vanessa's last night in town," Harley explained. "She's flying back to New York tomorrow afternoon. I think

I can get by without her nursing me anymore, though she's been a life-saver."

"Harley, it's been no trouble at all and you know it!" she protested.

"I wanted to show her a nice evening, so I booked us a limo. We took a long drive up the coast this afternoon, had champagne and watched the sunset from the top of Mount Tamalpais and then ate dinner with some old friends in Belvedere."

"An old beau of Harley's, it was. He was one of my dance students a hundred years ago," Vanessa said. "Someone phoned them after dinner and they said to turn on the news, so we heard all about what happened down here at the Men's cult. Harley and I had the same thought, that we had to come and try to find you, Tim."

Harley said, "Say, Tim... don't leave your friends on the sidewalk. Won't you boys join us?"

"Where are you going?" Barry asked, although he and Patrick were already climbing in over Vanessa's knees.

"To the Moscone Center," Harley said. "Where else?"

"Are you sure you're up for it, Harley?" Tim asked. "We don't have tickets."

"I wouldn't miss it for the world!" Harley said, lighting another joint. "Here...have a hit... and the tickets are on me."

The limousine pulled into the parking area off Howard Street. The banner that had been trailing the biplane over the city all week was now suspended between the flagpoles.

DANCE CELEBRATE REMEMBER
A Tribute to Sylvester's birthday
Moscone Center SATURDAY

The mirror ball Tim had first seen emerge from a bank of clouds above Twin Peaks as he sat on Harley's deck on Clementina Street was now suspended from a crane over the entrance. It splattered colored lights over Howard Street and their shoulders as they all went inside and rode the escalators down into the teeming dance floor.

Harley bought a round of drinks and they toasted to the demise of Arlo Montgomery. "I'll raise a glass to all of you boys," Vanessa said, "but I hate to think such an evil man was gay all along!"

"We don't call guys like him 'gay,' exactly," Patrick said. "He was a pervert, all right, but we don't want to claim a pederast who abuses young boys any more than the Catholics would want to claim him if he were a priest."

"Right on!" said Barry. "I was raised Catholic."

Harley and his sister found a perch at one side of the dance floor where they could see everything. Vanessa said, "This is a perfect spot and we can watch your jackets for you boys if you'd like to go dance. The line at the coat check area is a mile long."

Tim nearly forgot about Jason that evening. At least he didn't get around to finding the bar where Jason was working. The place was huge and Tim was too busy dancing! This was right where he wanted to be, in the center of the dancers at the core of the pulsing beat.

Barry, Tim and Patrick found their co-worker Jake on the dance floor and maneuvered toward him and his friends. Most of Jake's friends were bare-chested to show off their tattoos. Tim pulled off his white dess shirt and stuck it though one of the belt loops of his jeans as the DJ segued into Sylvester's old hit *Can't Stop Dancing!*

Groups of men caressed each another, pulled together and pushed apart, slapping asses like high school jocks in a locker room, all of them so hot and so high. Tim saw a sea of strangers and recognized some faces he'd seen around since the first day he arrived in San Francisco. At one point columns of smoke appeared across the middle of the dance floor, swirling from floor to ceiling. In the middle of each column a muscular man arose wearing a silver jockstrap and waving an enormous silver fan above his head. The fans moved the fog and the balloons and falling confetti. They reflected the colored lights in their folds as the fan dancers shook the sweat off their bodies.

Tim wouldn't criticize Vanessa's friends who created the spectacle for Arlo Montgomery's impressive arrival onto the stage at the "Men's Revival" meetings, but whoever designed the special effects for this party had them beat hands down! Tim wondered for a moment whether he was dreaming again as dozens of mirrored balls spun and dazzled above their heads.

There must have been thousands of men here, some of whom Tim had only seen on dance floors, many with whom he had shared more intimate moments, but there was nowhere in the world he had ever felt safer than right here in the middle of them. The "medicinal" marijuana that grew on Harley's South of Market deck had to be some of the best in the world or Tim was simply at the prime of his life. In this one rare moment of clarity he recognized and appreciated himself. He lost all track of time and danced as if there were no gravity, no floor beneath his feet. The rhythm matched his pulse and he became the melody. As stoned as he was, he also felt loved and embraced by the universe and he thought he now understood the ancient power of tribal drums.

Tim lifted his arms and closed his eyes. Someone reached around him from behind, tugged his nipples and ground his pelvis against Tim's ass. Tim looked down at the familiar hands and craned his neck to give Jean-Yves a wet kiss. Tim

closed his eyes again and another pair of hands covered Jean-
Yves' fingertips from in front. They slid down his sides and
pulled him into another man's hairy chest. It was Matthew, the
bartender from Harley's party last night. "Do you two know
each other?" Tim tried to ask, but the music was too loud to
talk and they just smiled. Matthew pulled Tim's face to his
own and pressed Tim's lips apart with his tongue. The three
of them moved as one with Tim sandwiched in the middle.

Tim loved the moment, but Jean-Yves and Matthew had a
big head start on this evening and Tim was sure he would see
them both another time. Tim wasn't in the mood for a three-
way—not tonight, anyway. The sexual energy was fantastic,
but his euphoria didn't even need it.

The news of Arlo Montgomery's demise must have
already spread through the Moscone Center. Even the most
apolitical men on the dance floor, those who took their
freedoms for granted, felt a sense that they were celebrating
something important. Tim had no idea how late it was when
he headed back to where he'd started. Patrick and Barry were
off somewhere dancing together and Tim watched Harley
standing, smiling, swaying to the music and staring across
the dance floor. Vanessa turned in time to see Tim reach for
his jacket in the pile. He mouthed "good-night" and "thanks"
and gave her a good-bye kiss on the cheek.

"Thanks for everything, Timothy Snow," Vanessa shouted
into his ear.

"But I didn't do anything, really."

"You and your friends brought down one of the monsters…
and besides, you introduced us to Artie Glamóur once again.
That alone would have been enough to thank you for."

"Thank you, Vanessa. Keep in touch." But Tim doubted
that he would ever see her again.

The DJ had just worked his way into Sylvester's *Lovin'
is really my Game* when Tim stepped onto the escalator. He
began his ascent to the street level while the music faded
away. It was time to go home now, even though this night had
reminded Tim of everything he loved about San Francisco.

He found a row of taxicabs out front and got in the first
one, startling the driver. "The Castro, please," Tim said and
pulled the door shut, "actually…Collingwood Street… near
twentieth."

"Hey, didn't I drop you off earlier?" It was the same driver
Tim had before.

"Yeah… small town, huh? How's it going tonight?"

"I had to deadhead back from the Excelsior district, so I
heard on the radio what happened at the Civic Center. They
finally nailed that mutha! Right on! Wish I coulda been there…
sounded like old times. How was the Sylvester reunion?"

"It was great—amazing, but it's time to go home. I've got
to work tomorrow."

The bars were long closed at this hour, but lines waited
outside the Bagdad Café and Orphan Andy's. A couple of dirty
young guys with cardboard signs asked for spare change or
cigarettes in front of the 24-hour Walgreens at 18th and Castro,
but even that corner was more quiet than usual.

Tim paid the driver and also gave him one of the joints
he found in his jacket pocket—Vanessa again. He wondered
if she'd done the same for Patrick and Barry. He would try to
remember to ask Patrick at work tomorrow. A lot of people
would be coming in with hangovers wanting eggs and Bloody
Marys and there was bound to be a late rush of customers
who'd slept in after dancing all night. As subtle as those
patterns were, people who worked in bars and restaurants
had them nearly memorized.

Tim also wanted to get his apartment in shape this week
before his Aunt Ruth arrived. Now he could begin to get

excited and look forward to her visit. He still needed a haircut and every inch of his apartment needed a good cleaning from top to bottom. But he was off Monday and Tuesday and if the fog burned back from the coast he could grab the morning paper, pick up a sandwich at Rossi's and head out to the beach for a quiet day by himself with one of Harley's joints.

Arturo had suggested to Tim that he get a hobby... besides men—so Tim wasn't surprised to find a stack of old paperbacks in the laundry room. Tim rifled through the ones on top and glanced at some of the titles: *Babycakes... Franny, Queen of Provincetown... The Front Runner... Men from the Boys... Dancer from the Dance*. Most of the books were old and well-worn, but judging from their covers, some of them might be right up Tim's alley.

The next time Tim went to Baker Beach or Land's End or San Gregorio he would stick one in his backpack and see if he liked it. If he wasn't in the mood for reading at the beach, he could take a walk on the paths and maybe run into another Corey out there—or maybe someone a little older. That cab driver with the ponytail last night was kind of hot. Guys like him had roots in the history of this town and they might be able to teach him something. As long as his HIV drugs kept working, Tim's world was wide open. Someone, maybe it was Jason, had once shown him where to look on the weather page of the Chronicle to check the tides under the Golden Gate Bridge. The lowest tide was when the beach would be its widest and he could have the most room to spread out, but he had to be careful not to fall asleep when the tide came back in. No matter how many amazing people came in and out of his life, whether they were lovers or mentors or friends or old ladies on the streetcar, no matter what else ever happened, there was no place he would rather be than San Francisco.

A sneak peek at
Chapter 1

from

Mark Abramson's

Cold Serial Murder

the sequel to
Beach Reading.

Chapter 1

"The first thing we should do, Aunt Ruth, is fire up a joint. We need to celebrate your arrival in San Francisco." Tim Snow reached for the ceramic Dalmatian next to the couch. He'd seen it at a yard sale and thought it tacky enough to be cute. The appeal was even greater when he brought it home and found a few stray buds and rolling papers under the secret lid.

He was thrilled to host the only family, by blood not by Castro, that he cared about. It had been years since he saw his Aunt Ruth. Of course, he couldn't remember the last time he'd entertained a houseguest for longer than one night. Does it count if you couldn't remember their names? "I'll roll us one while you get comfortable."

Ruth Taylor kicked off her shoes and rummaged through her carry-on bag for a pair of sandals. "I haven't smoked marijuana in ages. Not since my college days at Stanford."

"Trust me; it's like riding a bike." Tim didn't make the joint as thick as he normally liked, just in case. "Then I'll call Jason and see if he still wants to drive to San Gregorio this afternoon. It's a perfect day to put the top down on his convertible and head to the beach. If not, we can just walk over to Dolores Park for some sun. Are you hungry? I had a bowl of cereal earlier, but I could whip up some eggs and toast."

"No thanks. I bought a bagel in the Minneapolis airport that's still sitting on my stomach like a rock. Who's Jason, sweetie? Someone new in your life?"

"Oh, we're not like that anymore. But he does have a great car." Tim flicked the lighter. He was pleased that he could talk, could think, about Jason as a friend.

"What do you mean?"

"We went from boyfriends to *just friends* in less time than it takes some guys I know to pick out an outfit." Tim offered her the joint, but she was gazing out the window, not seeming to pay attention. "Are you okay?"

"Sorry, dear. I must be jet-lagged. I shouldn't be smoking pot, that's for sure. What were you saying about your friend?"

"He's a handsome guy, but I'm not the only one who thinks so. He can get anyone he wants. I'm glad we can be friends since we still have to work together."

"You're a very handsome guy, too, Tim."

"From an unbiased source, I'm sure." Tim took another hit off the joint and held it a while. "I'm just glad you could come and visit me. The last few months I've been picturing you working hard on Al Franken's Senate campaign, hosting a room full of rich Edina liberals, munching on organic crudités and sipping white wine."

"More coffee than wine, but you know, I liked him way back when he was on *Saturday Night Live* and I didn't even know he was political. Or that he was from Minnesota. But it's Obama that really got me excited in this election."

"Yeah, he's kinda hot if you like that skinny type, I guess." Tim took another hit off the joint and held it toward her.

"Maybe just a tiny puff, but don't you dare tell your cousin Dianne. She'll have her entire Bible class praying for me again. She thought they could pray me out of my divorce." Ruth pursed her lips and raised the joint to her mouth like she was taking a sip off a drinking straw.

"Now, don't get me wrong." A sudden cough broke her words. "We could all use the power of prayer now and then, but it seems to me that the people who are sure they have a direct line to heaven are most often calling collect with bad news."

She handed the joint back to Tim, stood up and took a couple of steps toward the window to stare out again and caught her reflection. She was amazed at how quickly the years had passed. *I'm 57 years old. It seems like only yesterday when I was just a college girl.* Her wedding announcement in the society pages of the *Minneapolis Star and Tribune* had read

Stanford Class of '73. How many other graduates had tried to cover the growing belly under their wedding dress with a bridal bouquet?

Ruth handed the joint back to Tim. "That tastes kind of nice. Brings back memories."

"How is dear cousin Dianne, anyway? I haven't seen her since we were kids."

"She was such a sweet baby, really. Now my bundle of joy is all big-haired Texas housewife who still thinks George Dubya Bush walks on water. I don't know where she gets it. I always knew she was rebellious, but I never dreamed she'd turn out this way. The last time we talked on the phone she cut me off because it was time to watch her favorite blowhard on Fox News. You can imagine what a disappointment she's been to me."

"If that's how she feels, I guess I'm beyond the help of her prayers."

"It's ridiculous. The whole world can be blowing up, but people want to fuss about gays getting married and same-sex couples raising kids. Plenty of children grow up well-adjusted with only one parent in this day and age. If two people love each other and can take good care of a child... aren't those kids better off than living in an orphanage? I've seen a lot of straight couples that were lousy parents."

"Like mine?"

"You turned out just fine, dear."

"You were always a bleeding heart, Aunt Ruth." Tim smiled up at her. "How did you and my mother turn out so different?"

"I don't know, Tim. We were like black and white ever since we were little girls. It's almost like you should have been my child and Dianne hers."

"I'm just glad you were there for me when my parents weren't. I would have dropped out of high school and run away after that fiasco with my track coach. I couldn't have spent one more night under their roof. I don't know what I would have done if you and Dan didn't take me in."

"Sometimes people just have to be there for each other, sweetheart." Ruth stretched. The pot left her feeling more restless than mellow. "Weren't you going to call your friend?"

"Oh yeah, I almost forgot." Tim reached for the phone and dialed and finally left a message. "Jason, it's Tim. Are you screening your calls? Pick up the phone. Where are you? My Aunt Ruth is here from Minneapolis... the one I told you about. Are we still on for that drive to the beach today? It should be hot at San Gregorio. Hello? Jason? Call me if you get back soon. It's about 10:30 now."

"What happened to your car, honey? The black Mustang on the Christmas card when your hair was curlier and longer?"

"It was always giving me trouble, so I sold it. Besides, you don't need a car in this city except to get *out* of the city. We can walk to Dolores Park from here. It looks like the fog has burned off and the view is great from the corner at the top. We can stop on Castro Street and pick up something to eat. I'm getting the munchies already."

They left the apartment on Collingwood and turned right past Spike's coffee shop, the barbers' and the dry cleaners. One of the coffee-drinkers seated on the sidewalk greeted Tim as they passed. When they crossed 19th Street someone honked and waved at him from a motorcycle.

On Castro Street, a tall blonde coming out of the plant store struggled with a ficus tree.

"Teresa!" Tim yelled. "Can I help you with that?"

"No thanks, darlin', the car is right here. Well, maybe you could shove those jumper cables over a little, thanks. Is this your Aunt Ruth?"

"Sure is. Aunt Ruth, I'd like you to meet my upstairs neighbor, Teresa. She's a teacher at the Harvey Milk School. Is this tree for your classroom?"

"No, silly. This is a gift for Lenny, my ex-husband. He's getting married, legal or not."

"Who to?"

"Teddy, that guy he met at Lazy Bear Weekend up at the Russian River last summer." Teresa made a face as she pinched a leaf. "I'd kill it for sure if I tried to grow it. I've never had any luck with ficus. My place is just as drafty as yours and the man at the plant store told me they don't do well in a draft. I hate to admit that I don't have a green thumb at all."

"Tell Lenny I said hi." Tim dusted whatever dirt from the pot clung to his palms. "And congratulations."

"I sure will. They're moving into a place in the Mission together. It has southern exposure and tons of windows, so all they need is plants. Between the two of them they have two of everything else. Two Cuisinarts, two blenders, two microwave ovens, and two of every cookbook Julia Child ever had a say in. What they need to have is a yard sale. Anyway, thanks, Tim. Nice to meet you, Ruth. Seeya later."

"My word, Tim! Do you know everyone in this city?" Ruth asked as she waved to Teresa.

"Not yet, but I'm working on it. It's a friendly neighborhood. Castro Street is just like the business district of any small town in America. Main Street, U.S.A. only a little more colorful, I'll give it that, and with better taste, for the most part. You should see it during Christmas. They put up a big tree across the street there in front of the bank and the stores and other businesses go all out. The decorations in the Castro are a lot less tacky than in most places."

Outside one of the 'adult novelty' stores two young men were smoking cigarettes. "Hey, Tim. How's it going? Did you get the trouble with your computer straightened out?"

"Yeah. Thanks, Marty. I called your friend Bob. He was terrific. Hey, Marty, this is my Aunt Ruth visiting from Minneapolis for a couple of weeks. Ruth, this is Marty. He works here. Be nice to him and you might get a discount on some souvenirs to take back home. The Jeff Stryker model would be a big hit with your Edina friends."

"I'm sure it would, dear." She glanced at the window display and then took a closer look. There were boxes with pictures of the male anatomy in ridiculous sizes, right out there in full view! *They would never get away with this in Minneapolis,* Ruth thought. *Not even on Hennepin Avenue.*

At Rossi's Deli they ordered sandwiches and cartons of salads and then headed across Castro toward the Twin Peaks bar. Ruth said, "This place looks cozy."

"The glass casket? I've heard that this was the first gay bar in town with windows onto the world outside – maybe the first in the country - way back in the seventies or something. We'll stop in there sometime. It's a good spot for people-watching."

They walked past the Castro Theatre and Ruth heard another, "Hiya, Tim" from a bleached-blonde girl in bib overalls coming out of Cliff's Hardware.

"Hey, Stella. Buying some new power tools?"

She laughed. "No, I've got all I need now, Tim. Who's the pretty lady?" More introductions were made and Ruth was starting to feel at home already.

Tim said, "Let's walk by Jason's house on our way to the park. He might have been out in the yard when I called."

They turned left on 18th Street and Ruth asked, "Where are we going, Tim? You said something about the beach, but the ocean is the other way. Am I turned around?"

"If Jason's not home we're going to the top of Dolores Park. It's a great place to sunbathe. You get all the same rays as at the beach without having to listen to that noisy surf!"

"Tim, I thought you loved the ocean. Isn't that why you moved to California?"

"I moved to California for the men, but the ocean was a close second. I love the beach. I'm just teasing you, Aunt Ruth. That's one of the things I love about you; you're so easy to tease."

"Well, I'm not stupid. I'm sure you're more comfortable around people you can relate to better than you could your family, myself excluded." Ruth sighed, "Tim, can we slow down a little? I'm not used to so much walking. These hills make me feel my age."

"Sorry, Aunt Ruth. Some days these hills make *me* feel your age. What are you now, anyway... thirty-five?"

"You're closer to thirty-five, dear. I have a daughter nearer to your age, remember?"

"I'm not even thirty, yet! My next birthday... maybe. You look great. My friend Renee could touch up your hair color and you'd look even better. Here's Jason's place. And there's his car in the driveway. He is too home. I thought so."

It was a 1965 cherry-red Thunderbird convertible with black interior. "Nice car, all right," Ruth said. "I've always wanted a convertible, but they're so impractical in the Midwest. They rust out before they can wear out and there just aren't enough days when you want to ride around with the top down. It's too cold in the winter and in the summertime in Minnesota you definitely want a car with air conditioning." Ruth was admiring what great shape the car was in while Tim ran ahead down the driveway and around to the back door of Jason's house.

Ruth looked down and saw bright shiny pools of red on the ground as if the car had just been sloppily painted right there in the driveway. But the red on the ground was a few shades darker than the Thunderbird's paint color and it looked like it was still wet. That was when she heard her nephew scream.

TO BE CONTINUED...

Like Tim Snow, Mark Abramson grew up in Minnesota and also worked for a time as a waiter in the Castro, but is better known as a bartender and producer of events such as "Men Behind Bars" and big dance parties on the San Francisco piers, "Pier Pressure" and "High Tea." He also had an Aunt Ruth Taylor, but his maternal grandmother was not a psychic. His other grandmother might have been, but she died before he was born. And his mother doesn't drink at all, unfortunately.

Mark Abramson's writing has appeared in the gay press as far back as *Christopher Street* magazine, *Gay Sunshine, Mouth of the Dragon* and *Fag Rag* and more recently in the Lethe Press anthology *Charmed Lives: Gay Spirit in Storytelling*. In addition to the Beach Reading series, he is working on his Castro Street diaries which recount true tales of life before AIDS in the great gay Mecca with friends such as John Preston, Rita Rockett, Randy Shilts and Al Parker.

Coming Soon
from Lethe Press

THE BEACH READING SERIES

Beach Reading

Cold Serial Murder

Russian River Rat

Snowman

Wedding Season

Neutriva Dreams

Love Rules

LaVergne, TN USA
06 June 2010
185162LV00001B/9/P